PRAISE FOR
THERE'S NO BASE LIKE HOME

"Ahh, how I wish I had this book by Jessica and Alana back in middle school. All I wanted to do was fit in and NOT BE NOTICED. It wasn't until later in college that I came to love my awkwardness and own my awesome (or awkward). :) When you embrace what is different, the world suddenly opens up in the most magical way."

—**Julie Foudy**, two-time FIFA Women's World Cup champion and Olympic gold medalist

"*There's No Base Like Home*: a perfect title with a beautiful message authored by two women who have clearly found their "home base" within. There is strength in uniqueness. . . . This is timely and timeless."

—**Kerri Walsh Jennings**, three-time Olympic gold medalist and professional beach volleyball player

"I thoroughly enjoyed *There's No Base Like Home*! It brought me back to the adventures, fun, and adversity of my childhood playing the game I love. I love the message encouraging athletes to find their strengths and not being afraid to stand out!"

—**Jennie Finch**, two-time Olympic softball pitcher

"In this story of stepping outside the box, Jessica Mendoza and her sister Alana have written a delightful, female-driven sports story about a young girl following her dreams and not being afraid to stand out. I was rooting for awesome Sophia and her whole familia from the first pitch. Go Sophie, go!"

—**Pablo Cartaya**, Pura Belpré Award Honor-winning author of *The Epic Fail of Arturo Zamora*

THERE'S NO BASE
like
Home

THERE'S NO BASE like Home

by **JESSICA MENDOZA**
and **ALANA MENDOZA DUSAN**

illustrated by
RUTH MCNALLY BARSHAW

TU BOOKS
An imprint of LEE & LOW BOOKS Inc.
New York

Text copyright © 2018 by Pretty Tough, LLC
Illustrations copyright © 2018 by Ruth McNally Barshaw

TU BOOKS, an imprint of LEE & LOW BOOKS Inc., 95 Madison Avenue, New York, NY 10016
leeandlow.com

Manufactured in the United States of America by Worzalla Publishing Company

MIX
Paper from
responsible sources
FSC® C002589

Book design by Christy Hale
Book production by The Kids at Our House
The text is set in Today Sans Serif Regular
The illustrations are rendered in ink-filled brush pen
10 9 8 7 6 5 4 3 2 1
First Edition

Library of Congress Cataloging-in-Publication Data

Names: Mendoza, Jessica (Sports analyst), author. | Dusan, Alana Mendoza, author. | Barshaw, Ruth McNally, illustrator.
Title: There's no base like home / Jessica Mendoza and Alana Mendoza Dusan ; illustrated by Ruth McNally Barshaw.
Description: First edition. | New York : Tu Books, an imprint of Lee & Low Books Inc., 2018. | Series: Peace, love, and softball ; book 1 | Summary: Sophia Garcia, twelve, wants to excel at softball like her older sister, Ellie, and make her family proud, but when she is chosen for a different team and position than Ellie, she must learn to succeed by being herself.
Identifiers: LCCN 2017058032| ISBN 9781620145883 (hardcover : alk. paper) | ISBN 9781620145906 (mobi)
Subjects: | CYAC: Softball—Fiction. | Sisters—Fiction. | Self-confidence—Fiction. | Family life—California—Fiction. | Hispanic Americans—Fiction. | California—Fiction.
Classification: LCC PZ7.1.M4714 The 2018 | DDC [Fic]—dc23
LC record available at https://lccn.loc.gov/2017058032

To Mom and Dad—
for always being our number-one
fans in softball and in life.

To our Mendoza family—
for surrounding us with love, culture, and
plenty of hugs and kisses.

To our children and all dreamers
out there—
find what makes you different
and STAND OUT instead of
blending in. The magic happens when
you become what few others are
willing to be.
—Jessica & Alana

To my many sisters
—R.M.B.

AUTHOR'S NOTE

Dear Reader,

One of the hardest things to do in life is to figure out who you are. What makes you different? What allows you to STAND OUT? The easiest path is to try to fit in, to be like those around you—or like those you see on TV. Look like this, treat people like that, dress this way, and have the same goals as others.

However, I've found that the best experiences in life—and the most fun you'll ever have—come from stepping outside the box. Competing in the Olympics was one of the coolest things I ever experienced. Now, working with Major League Baseball as a TV analyst for ESPN, as one of very few women in the field, has been one of the hardest yet best things I've ever done. None of these things would have been possible had I not learned how to stand out.

I remember as a young girl always trying to fit in, picking the wrong friends at first, hiding my passion for playing softball. But then I started noticing strong female role models who were successful: Olympians, college athletes, even a local athlete who had a full scholarship for softball. They were different, and they were unafraid of being different. I made a change in my life and surrounded myself with people who got me. I found myself smiling when I didn't have to act, or dress, or say the same things as others, because I knew that staying true to my own passions and beliefs would lead me to stand out and be successful.

In this book, Sophia Garcia takes a similar journey. She is a young girl exploring all the unique aspects of her own life. She faces the challenges we all face as girls, from the judgment of others to the beauty and hardships that come from competing in sports. Through it all is the one constant as we grow and figure it all out: family.

My sister Alana and I wrote *There's No Base Like Home* to give all young girls more confidence to stay true to who they are. We hope they make better decisions from it and ultimately stand out to become the strongest, smartest, and most successful versions of themselves.

Jessica Mendoza

Introduction

This is going to be the best year ever. I just turned twelve, I have the best family, I play the best sport, and I'm starting middle school! First things first. Let me introduce myself and my family.

On the top left is my dad, Louie Garcia. Everyone knows him because of his horseshoe-shaped mustache. It gives him a conquistador vibe that's intimidating to some of the neighborhood kids, but really, he's the nicest guy ever. The funny thing is, he's had the 'stache since before I was born, and I'm not sure I would even recognize him if he shaved it off.

Whenever he says, "I mustache you a question," and twirls his legendary whiskers, I collapse in giggles.

Two years ago, Dad got a job as a security guard at a corporate office building. We were all excited for him, but sad at the same time because he works so much now. He used to spend hours after school and on weekends playing sports with me and my sister, and had time to coach us on our softball teams. His current job doesn't mean he can't coach us—he still does, just not officially.

Maybe it's because I'm the baby of the family, but Dad and I have a special bond. We understand each other. I'm a classic daddy's girl.

On the top right is my mom, Maria. To me, she looks like an angel. She has a beauty that radiates her kind soul. Mom is my safe haven. When the world crashes down, I lie next to her and she lets me Kim K ugly-cry all over her lap. Most of the time she doesn't need to say anything—her presence is like a magic potion.

On the bottom left is my older sister Ellie, who is a freshman at Moorpark High. She's brutally honest, like pretty much every member of the Garcia family. Sometimes I avoid asking Ellie for advice for exactly that reason.

Ellie is the best at a lot of things. She's really smart and always gets good grades—but more than that, she's the best softball player I know. We spend most of our time together practicing at the elementary school around the corner from our house.

Yesterday was one of those days.

"Pump the umph!" Ellie yelled, using the deepest voice she could. She was doing her best impression of Dad, which made us both giggle. The word "umph" came from one of his many sayings, or "Dadisms" as we call them.

Some of the Dadisms are trite—some of them even make us want to roll our eyes—but most of the time, they're full of such good advice that we have no choice but to listen. One of Dad's favorite Dadisms, the one he says all the time, especially during softball season, is that "the difference between *try* and *triumph* is just a little *umph*."

UMPH

In his eyes, "umph" is the difference between being good and being great. We turned it into our own secret catchphrase. It's an insider joke reminding us to do our very best.

And then there's me, Sophia Maria Garcia. Yeah, the one with the funky hair. I didn't get my mom's thick, long, beautiful hair like Ellie. I got these crazy curls that never do what I want them to, so I wear them up all the time. I only notice how long my hair is when it's wet after a shower, before it dries and curls up again.

My favorite things to do are play softball, hang out with my family, and watch movies like *The Wizard of Oz*. Mom said starting sixth grade and going to middle school will be an adventure, more exciting than Dorothy's, so she gave me this journal to document it all. I'm a little nervous about all the changes, but I guess we'll see how it goes.

August 25 • TRAINING ZONE

This weekend will be the most important of my life. The Waves are having tryouts, and they're one of the best 12U softball teams in Southern California. Ellie played for them the year they won the national championship. They helped develop her into the player she is today—most likely the starting pitcher for the Moorpark Mustangs varsity team *as a freshman*. Scouts sometimes come to tournaments just to watch her pitch. She's definitely going to play in college and maybe beyond.

Me? I'm still finding my way around a base path. We've both been playing since we were old enough to throw a ball, but Ellie is almost three years older, so she's had a lot more practice. Not that she needs it. Ellie is a natural. She can fire a fastball at almost sixty mph. She can also pick up a bat and knock the ball right out of the park. It took me literally hundreds of at bats before I finally sent one flying over the fence.

I love pitching, like Ellie. Striking a batter out is one of the best feelings in the world, and ever since I watched her first game with the Waves, I have wanted to follow in her footsteps.

Today we loaded up the car with our softball gear—two buckets of balls, our bat bags, a batting tee, video camera and tripod, and a huge mesh screen, which we transported on the roof of our car. While Dad drove, Mom, Ellie, and I each rolled down our window and held the screen tight so it didn't fly off. Good thing we were just going around the corner, because I'm pretty sure carrying that thing on the top of our car isn't legal. We didn't need the screen when Ellie and I were younger, but since we're stronger hitters now, Dad built the screen to protect himself when he pitches to us in batting practice (BP).

The elementary school has a baseball diamond—more like a grassy area with a rusty chain-link backstop and faded base paths, but at least it's a place where we can practice. While Dad set up his video camera, Ellie and I warmed up, tossing the ball back and forth.

When he's not at work, Dad videotapes every practice and game and breaks it down with us afterward. We appreciate the feedback . . . but sometimes we have to remind him we're not Major League ballplayers.

Dad likes to practice gamelike situations, so he has pretend hitters and pitch counts. He's trying to teach us which pitches to throw at which times. I got into pitching position and spun the ball on my hip, waiting for him to give me a sign. I like smacking my glove on my thigh—it makes a really cool popping sound when I release the ball. It's good for special effects, but leaves a huge welt on my leg.

"Ellie, you're up!" Dad instructed.

She stepped into the left-side batter's box and held an imaginary bat.

"All right, we have a lefty!" he announced. "She could be good at short game, or she could be a long-ball hitter. Let's start low and away and see what she does." Dad called for a drop ball outside.

I brought my hands together, spun the ball around in my glove to find my grip, and took a series of deep breaths.

"Let's see what you got," Ellie said with a wink. I smiled back and then fired. She stepped toward the ball but held her swing and let the pitch pass.

"Strike!" Dad yelled. "Okay, Sophia. What did you learn?"

"She's not slapping or bunting. She wants to hit away and doesn't really like outside pitches, since she didn't go for one low and away." A half grin crept over my face as I tried to hide how proud of myself I was.

"Not bad. Not bad. So now what pitch do you think would be good?" Dad wants me to build up my instincts.

"Maybe a curveball inside?" I suggested.

"Okay, let's try it."

This time Ellie took a huge imaginary swing and almost fell on her butt. "Ahaha!" I shouted to Ellie. "Gotcha!"

"Game face, Sophia. Practice won't help you in the game unless you treat practice *like* a game."

"If I had a real bat, that would've been over the fence anyway," Ellie added.

"This *is* a real game. Come on, Ellie. Game face."

Both Ellie and I had to suppress our laughter. Nothing cracks us up more than mocking Dad. Poor guy. ☺

"All right, girls. That's enough. What next?" he questioned.

"Another curveball," I said. "This time she might fall all the way over."

"Don't be overconfident. What's the count now?" Dad asked.

"No balls, two strikes."

"Like Ellie said, there's a possibility you got lucky with the first curveball. She might connect with the next one and send it over the fence."

Of course, Ellie loved that comment. She hit an imaginary

home run and began running the bases with her hands up in the air, triumphant.

"You never want to give up a good hit when the count is 0–2. That's when you throw what we call a waste pitch: a pitch that's out of the strike zone that the batter may or may not swing at, but definitely not something she could get the barrel of the bat on. Why don't we go with a backdoor curveball or a drop ball outside?"

"Okay. Let's do a curveball outside."

I took a deep breath and fired, hoping to catch the back corner—or backdoor—of the plate. Ellie took a check swing and brought her imaginary bat back, taking the pitch for a ball. The count was now 1–2. One ball. Two strikes.

"Now what're you thinking?" Dad asked as he tossed the ball back to me. "How are you going to get her to make a mistake?"

I knew what Dad was hinting at. Hitters often chase pitches that are out of the strike zone. His advice to us when we're batting: *Never chase pitches because it will lead to mistakes. If you're not looking for the changeup, don't swing at it unless you get two strikes.*

"A changeup," I responded with confidence, visualizing the slow-moving pitch. It can catch a hitter off guard because the speed is so much slower than a normal pitch that it throws them off-balance.

"All right, let's see it."

I took a deep breath, found my grip, and wound up. I was cognizant of my arm speed to not give the pitch away. It floated in and dropped just below Ellie's imaginary bat as she swung and missed.

8

"Oh, no! I've lost the game. Awwhuhuhu." Ellie fell to her knees and began pretend-weeping.

"Nice pitch. A little too much over the plate, though. It needs to be outside. If you get it over the plate, even if she's off-balance, she can still get a good piece of it."

The smile on my face from watching Ellie's performance melted away. "But I struck her out, Dad! Why do you have to focus on the negative?"

"Sophia, she doesn't even have a bat in her hand. She *might* have hit it. You did good, but you could do better. Do you think Olympic players get there because they're okay with just being good? NO! They push themselves to be better. To be the best!"

"Okay, Dad. I get it, I get it. I can always be better."

Did he know he was talking to a twelve-year-old? I mean, I haven't even started high school yet, and he's talking Olympics!

The three of us finished up a few more "innings" of imaginary, situational at bats before Ellie started real batting practice. While she hit, I headed to the outfield to shag balls. Even though I don't play outfield, that's where I position myself because Ellie hits left-handed and always sends ball to right field and right center.

I must have been really motivated today, because when Ellie hit one down the right field line, my mind traveled a lot faster than my legs. I took off toward the line, and somehow I thought leaving the ground would help. I laid

out, diving for the ball, but still came up short as my body slid along the surface of the field. So I lay on the ground, enjoying the relief of the cool grass.

Then Dad yelled from the pitcher's mound. "You just gave up a triple!"

"What?"

"By diving down the line. If that were a game, that easily would have been a triple. That's Outfield 101. Never dive down the line."

"Okay, Dad," I responded. At the same time, I thought, *I don't even play outfield! Ellie and I are pitchers. It's not like it's my job to worry about it.*

I glanced over at Ellie, who tried to refrain from laughing. I bet *she* was thinking, *Better her than me!*

August 25 • THE NIGHT BEFORE TRYOUTS

Dinner is a big deal in our house. It isn't a particularly fancy meal, or even a long meal, but everyone sits down at the table together, and the only real rule is that there are absolutely no screens at the table. Just good food and good family. (Yep, that is another Dadism.)

Before I sit down to eat every night, I turn my attention to my favorite bowl in the house: the fishbowl. We have two orange clown fishes named Anna and Elsa, and a small white fish with brown stripes named Olaf. I can never decide which fish is my favorite. I watched them chomp ocean-blend seaweed flakes for a while before Mom called everyone to the table.

We each have a regular seat in the dining room. Ellie sits across from Mom, next to me. I sit across from Dad. Our family is very balanced. I like that. No matter what bad thing may happen during the day, I fit in at home. Even if girls are mean at school, or I hate my hair, my seat at the table always makes me feel just right. I hope I'm ready to fit in somewhere else too.

I hope it will be on the Waves.

"So are you ready for tryouts, Sophia?" Dad asked, mixing random condiments to season his rice.

"I hope so! I felt good practicing today, so hopefully that carries over," I said, trying to convince myself as much as the rest of the family.

"You're going to crush it!" Ellie whispered to me with a mouth full of shredded chicken.

"Ellie!" Mom interrupted. "Eat, then talk." She's a real stickler for manners.

"You'll be fine," Ellie continued.

My heart beat quicker just thinking about tomorrow. I *knew* I'd be fine. I'd only been practicing for this since I was five! But I didn't feel that confident. Maybe the problem was that for the first time in my life, "fine" might not be good enough. Fine may be okay for T-ball or rec ball, but this was travel ball, where all the best players play.

I needed to be better than fine. I needed to be great.

I *needed* to make the team.

And just then Dad said, "You'll be better than fine," as if he knew that was exactly what I needed to hear.

⚾

We all share a bathroom in our house—well, we're supposed to share, but Ellie complains I hog it. My electric toothbrush was buzzing over my teeth as I stood in front of the sink, getting ready for bed. Still wet from the shower, my hair was tied into a big mess of a bun on top of my head.

"What's taking so long?" Ellie yelled.

She had already brushed her teeth and washed up. "What's all the fuss about?" I asked. "You don't need—"

"Unlock the door. I need to give you something."

I was intrigued, so I opened the door. She stood there smiling, then hung a baseball cap on top of my bun. She hung it backward, so all I could see in the mirror was that the hat was black, but I knew exactly what it was. It was Ellie's first Waves hat.

"For good luck," Ellie said.

The hat was dirty and sweaty and weathered, but it looked good on me. I looked like a real softball player. The only way a hat looked like that was if you played hundreds of games wearing it. I hope I get to wear it in a hundred more games.

The bill of the cap was a deep ocean blue, and there was a matching blue wave on the front. It would perfectly match my blue shoelaces.

Lying in bed, I couldn't stop thinking a million thoughts. I'm used to my thoughts racing, but it felt like they were jumping and spinning, having a dance party in my brain.

What if I don't make the team? What if I'm not actually good enough? The last thing I want to do is disappoint my parents—and Ellie. I especially do not want to disappoint Ellie, who has been my idol and role model for as long as I can remember.

I turned over my pillow, pressing the cooler side against my cheek. I hoped it would slow down my thoughts. It didn't. But it did move them forward. I saw myself stepping out on the field at tryouts. I saw the coaches and the other girls and the bats and the balls . . . Even in my imagination, it felt like so much fun. It felt like all I ever wanted.

And I realized that the person I *especially* don't want to disappoint is myself.

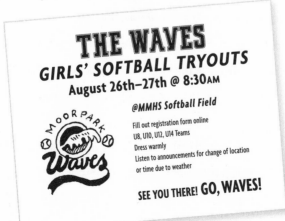

THE WAVES
GIRLS' SOFTBALL TRYOUTS
August 26th–27th @ 8:30AM

@MMHS Softball Field

Fill out registration form online
U8, U10, U12, U14 Teams
Dress warmly
Listen to announcements for change of location
or time due to weather

SEE YOU THERE! GO, WAVES!

August 26 • WAVES TRYOUTS, DAY 1

On the morning of tryouts, Mom made chorizo-and-egg burritos before she and Ellie left for Panthers practice. The Panthers are Ellie's travel team, and she practices with them three to four times a week. Normally I would *devour* a breakfast burrito, but today I couldn't bring myself to eat. My stomach was in knots, and I wasn't sure if I was going to throw up or pee my pants!

Sitting in Dad's old Ford pickup on the way to the field, I couldn't stop my leg from bouncing real fast like the piston of an engine.

"You don't need to be nervous," Dad said.

"What makes you think I'm nervous?" I was coolness itself.

Yeah, right.

"Okay. You're not nervous." Dad smiled, watching my leg shake intensely.

We both bounce our legs when we're anxious. It's our way of keeping pace with the thoughts whirling in our brains.

I chewed on my fingernail. "Really, I'm fine. Just excited," I lied.

Dad just nodded. He can read me like a book.

As we pulled into the parking lot, I saw a bunch of girls and their parents getting gear out of their cars. A lot of hands on shoulders and last-minute words of wisdom. A lot of stoic faces ready for battle. I glanced at my still-uneaten breakfast burrito, which I'd brought with me. If I'd eaten it, maybe my stomach wouldn't have room for so many butterflies.

"Do you want me to walk you over to the dugout?" Dad asked hopefully.

"No, thanks. I'll be fine. I'm good. Thanks," I repeated, mostly to assure myself. I rubbed my fingers over the lettering of Ellie's hat and visualized myself in a complete Waves uniform.

"You *sure* you don't want me to walk you over?" Dad asked again. I guess he was feeling some nerves too.

"I'm good," I said again, more confidently this time. I wanted to make a solid first impression.

As I walked to the dugout with my bat bag slung over my shoulder, I didn't see other dads or moms walking their kids over. I'd made the right choice. But there were tons of parents perched on their folding chairs down the first and third baselines. Some of them appeared more anxious than their daughters.

All I could focus on was the Waves coach and all the prospective new players. There were *so* many players. I tore a hanging cuticle off with my teeth.

Dad came up behind me and whispered, "Fake it till you make it!"

I turned and gave him a smile. He always says that to Ellie and me when we feel intimidated. We need to tell ourselves we're the best players in the world. We need to have the game face of the best player—the walk, the hype, the confidence of the best player. And even though we might be faking it, we keep faking it until we make it.

Once a player makes the Waves, she stays on the team until

she ages out. This year in particular, lots of girls were coming back for another season. There were only three open spots—and at least *thirty* girls trying to fill them.

The Waves are a dynasty, and no matter how few open spots, there will always be more players trying to make the team. I need to make sure I'm one of the best.

Ellie can make friends anywhere, anytime, whereas I sometimes get tongue-tied talking to myself. In order to look busy, I hooked my bat bag on the fence and double-knotted my blue laces. I'd already tied them—and rechecked—before I left the car, but I wanted to be certain I was ready to go. I held my hands behind my back to keep from biting my nails.

Behind me, someone shouted, "Hey!" I spun around. "I'm Teresa." It was a cheerful girl wearing a neon pink tank. Her voice was a little too loud and a little too excited. It sounded like the voice inside my head. Teresa's shoulder-length sun-streaked hair was split into two separate braids. When she smiled, she had a mouthful of braces, and the rubber bands in her mouth matched her tank top. Color coordination seemed important to her.

It felt like I'd swallowed a frog as my heart beat loudly in my neck. I was stressing so much about how to be social that when a social opportunity presented itself, I couldn't find words.

Speak, you idiot! Say something! I finally blurted out my name.

"That's a pretty name. What position do you play?" she replied in a chipper, high-pitched voice.

"Um"—still struggling to get words out—"pitcher."

"Me too!" My heart immediately stopped. I took a deep breath. My first chance at making a team friend, and we were competing against each other?

Unfazed, she asked, "Where'd you get that hat?"

I reached up and touched my cap, a half smile coming to my face as I remembered my excitement. "My sister."

"Lucky."

I knew she meant I was lucky to have the hat, but I couldn't help thinking I was really lucky to have my sister, too. "Yeah."

"So then you'll definitely make the team."

"Oh, no! Don't jinx it!" I knocked on my hat. My mom has a habit of knocking on her head whenever she says something she doesn't want to stick, as if she is knocking on wood and the action will chase bad luck away. It never made sense to me, but I find myself doing it more and more.

"I'm just calling it like I see it. I always call it like that."

That comment made me giggle because my family is known for being blunt. If that's how Teresa is too, we'd get along just fine.

"Do you want to warm up together?" She got up on her tiptoes, as if her words themselves did not provide the amount of energy she required.

"Um, sure." She had a nice, friendly vibe. Her easy smile helped calm my nerves. There is nothing worse than feeling like you're the one person no one wants to pick as their partner. All I had to worry about was keeping up with everything she said. In the short warm-up period, I learned Teresa's whole life story as well as her schedule of classes, her favorite subjects, and how much she disliked mayonnaise.

Between throws, I wondered how good of a pitcher she was. Warming up her arm, she threw some serious darts.

Even though I was slightly distracted by my dry mouth and sweaty hands, I was in the right place. Sometimes I'm too silly or too self-conscious. But on the softball field, everything feels just right. I had a super good feeling about tryouts.

I knocked on my Waves cap again just to be sure.

After warm-ups, players split into their respective positions. Most of the girls were infielders. Players heading to the outfield were probably really good hitters who didn't play defense well, or really fast and able to run down balls.

Pitchers and catchers gathered in the batting cages. I've been pitching the last three seasons on my all-star team, so I joined them, fingers crossed behind my back. There were five girls with me, but besides Teresa, I didn't learn their names. I didn't have time to make friends. I needed to focus. The presence of the Waves' starting pitcher, Amanda, made me even more nervous. Her return to the team meant one less opening for a pitcher.

Ellie and I have been pegged as pitchers since we started playing. At least, Ellie has. She's always been tall for her age, which gives her an advantage because her long arms and legs allow her to generate speed. I mostly followed her example. I don't have her height, but I'm a pretty good little pitcher.

I followed the other rookies, nervously rubbing a thumb on the leather of my glove. Each of us got paired with a catcher.

"Hi, I'm Kim," my catching partner said. Kim Cheung was the Waves' catcher from last year, and a solid player from what I've seen. Her stick-straight hair, the color of coal, was pulled into a long ponytail beneath her cap, which she wore backward to accommodate her catcher's mask.

"Sophia," I responded with a nervous smile. I didn't want to tell her I remembered her, or that Ellie was my sister. Being related to Ellie is a double-edged sword. Sometimes I carry her shine and bask in her glow; other times a certain expectation sets in that I'm not sure I can live up to.

"So how do you like to warm up?" Kim asked.

"Um . . ." The rubbing of my glove escalated. My mind went blank.

"Like, do you need to throw overhand more or . . ."

My brain finally kicked into gear. " Jim, I think I'll just take a knee and work on my spins." I tossed ball with my fingertips, controlling the rotation.

"Okay." Kim looked relieved I had some idea what I was doing. Taller and much stronger than me in build, she hopped behind home plate. She looked so experienced, which made me question my appearance. Who would want a tiny little pitcher so nervous she's rubbing a hole in her glove?

Kim smacked her fist into her mitt and put it up as a target, snapping me back to reality. After about fifteen minutes, my arm was loose.

Coach Adam called out, "Listen up! We're going to rotate players in so everyone has a chance to pitch and hit." His worn baseball cap covered his slightly balding head, and he had a dollop of zinc on his sunburned nose. He had been an assistant coach when Ellie was on the team, and I wondered if he remembered me.

As we moved into the dugout, I watched other pitchers throw. The girls who already played a season with the team seemed so confident and relaxed. What would it be like to be one of them?

A shout from Coach Adam interrupted my daydream. "Sophia Garcia!" He referred to his clipboard. "Your turn!" My name didn't seem to register with him, which triggered mixed feelings. Did he *know* I was Ellie's sister? Did he care?

I stepped up to the pitcher's rubber—a rectangular area on the mound—and my legs turned to Jell-O. I closed my eyes, and when I opened them, instead of seeing the catcher's glove as my target, I saw a tall, dark-haired girl step into the batter's box and glare intently at me—she had her game face on.

Kim crouched behind home plate, signaling for a fastball by pointing her mitt down and flicking it up. The ball took a few turns in my hand as I struggled to find the grip. I tried to throw quickly so it didn't seem like I was stalling, but when I felt the snap of the ball upon release, I knew I didn't get as much spin on it as I was hoping for. A second later, bang. Game Face Girl hit a solid shot right to midfield. It took one hop and bounced off the shoulder of Becky, a scrappy girl trying out for second base. Becky's eyes followed the ball into the outfield, and when she turned back around, I spotted a look of discouragement on her face. I bet we were mirror images of each other. Both of us were losing confidence.

The next hitter, a stocky red-haired girl with a face full of freckles and a ton of nervous energy, stepped up to the plate, and Kim signaled for a curveball. My heart almost stopped when the pitch went flat. Thank goodness it was low and Freckle Face didn't swing. Ball one. The next call was for a changeup. Risky, but worth it if thrown correctly. It has to be slow enough and low and outside to effectively throw a hitter off-balance.

Snap. Too high this time. Freckle Face was a little unsteady, but when she unleashed her hands, she sent the ball into the gap between left and center field. I tracked it as far as I could. Then, as the ball started to drop, the Waves' starting left fielder, Olivia Jenkins, easily made the catch.

My cheeks burned after allowing another hard shot, but I tried to brush it off—literally wiping my red cheeks with my forearms—before stepping back on the mound. I needed to pitch a strike and redeem myself. I visualized the ball sailing over home plate in the zone between the batter's knees and shoulders with enough speed and spin to make her swing and miss.

Boom. The steely-eyed batter nailed my pitch, and Olivia got another crack at a fly ball. It sailed high and far into the left-center gap again.

Olivia sprinted after it, **s-t-r-e-t-c-h-e-d** her whole body . . . and **DOVE** to catch the ball before it landed in the grass.

Ugh. Maybe Teresa *had* jinxed things.

Tryouts were definitely not going according to plan. Hitter after hitter, I rushed. Pitch after pitch, my throws were either flat or missed the mark. My palms were sweaty, and my hands shook. I couldn't catch my breath. Dad always tells me that pitching is more mental than physical, but it was impossible to control my mind.

As I stomped off the field during the next switch-out, I looked at Becky, who was staring at the ground. She definitely wasn't fielding as clean as she had started the day. We were both worried.

I heard a familiar whistle. It was Dad. My heart leapt, initially comforted by seeing him. But that feeling was quickly replaced with anxiety over disappointing him. He's put so much effort into coaching me, and I didn't want him to think it's been a waste of time.

"Sophia, being nervous is normal." He took me aside. "Try Ellie's routine. It helps her focus. Just concentrate on steady breathing. Big inhale. Big exhale. Forget where you are, who your opponent is, and just focus on the ball."

"Thanks, Dad." I put on a brave face and stifled the sob caught in my throat.

When it was my turn to hit, I tried Ellie's hitting routine. I held up my bat and spun it around to the label. I took a deep breath and stared at the stamped logo. As I exhaled, the rest of the world melted away. Even though I throw right-handed, I hit left. Dad always says I'm two steps closer to first base that way. I touched the bat to the plate and stepped in with my left foot, followed by my right. Then I pointed the bat directly at Amanda, the Waves' pitcher, challenging her. *I dare you to throw it anywhere near the strike zone.*

The first pitch was a ball outside. With the second throw, Amanda tried to come into my kitchen, and I smoked a foul ball down the first baseline.

"¡Otra vez!" Dad yelled from the sidelines. Basically telling me, *You're on it! Do it again!*

I focused on the next pitch, and saw more hand than ball, meaning it was most likely an off-speed pitch. It was risky, but since I had one ball and one strike, I could sit on the pitch in case she threw a changeup.

Did that pay off! As the pitch floated in, I sat back and nailed the ball into the right-center gap. I ran my heart out and slid safely into second on a huge wave of accomplishment.

Day One with the Waves: ✔

August 27 • WAVES TRYOUTS, DAY 2

I wasn't sure what Day Two of tryouts would bring, and I wanted to start the day off right, so I did my best to get some food in my stomach. We all took a knee in the grass when Coach Adam called us over. Teresa slid up next to me. All superstitions aside, I was happy to see a friendly face and didn't *really* think she'd jinxed me.

Coach Adam has been around the game for ages and coached both his daughters—one of whom is on scholarship at Oregon State. He spends all his spare time on the field, scouting and mentoring girls he thinks have skills. Ellie says Coach Adam is known for his intensity. His expectations are high, and each player desperately does not want to disappoint him. His motto is that all is fair in love and softball—if you can't step up, then you can sit down . . . on the bench.

Once we settled down, Coach Adam launched into a pep talk. "Great softball teams aren't just built with athletes, but with mental toughness," he began. I've heard it all from Dad *many* times. Coach Adam's voice went gruff. "To be the best means no one can be complacent. You have to push yourself every day knowing that if you aren't cutting it, there's someone ready to take your place. So it's important for us to select players who push themselves hard every day."

As he scanned the prospective players, he added, "We also pride ourselves on team spirit! So I'm going to ask our returning players to show you what I mean." He stepped aside, and eight girls lined up, wearing their black-and-blue practice jerseys. Most wore braids in their hair. Some even had eye black under their eyes.

I didn't know all the players' names, but I recognized Kristy Major, team captain and starting center fielder, from when she played with Ellie. Kristy was such a strong hitter she made the team as a *ten*-year-old, which is almost unheard of. This was going to be her third season with the Waves.

Bouncing, Kristy brushed her bangs from her eyes and led the team in a cheer.

Kristy: *We are the Waves.*

Team: *Rock the boat!*

Kristy: *We're feeling fine!*

Team: *Rock the boat!*

Kristy (louder): *You mess with us,*

Team: *Rock the boat!*

Kristy (even louder): *We'll blow your mind!*

Team (yelling in rhythm): *We said bang, bang, choo-choo train, wind me up, and we'll do our thing. We know karate, we know kung fu, you mess with us—and we'll mess with you!*

The girls clapped, slowly at first—*clap, clap, clap, clap*—then built into everyone clapping as fast as they could and stomping their feet furiously.

I loved the cheering. It took all my self-control not to sing along when they got to the "choo-choo train" part. I knew all the words from when Ellie was on the team.

At the end of the cheer, we were definitely pumped. Kristy was jumping up and down and high-fiving Olivia, who sat next to her. The two returning players had a bond.

"All right!" Coach Adam continued. "Like I said, we pride ourselves on having team players, so today let's see how you play at different positions."

I was relieved not to have the pressure of pitching again and jogged over to second base. Coach warmed us up by hitting routine ground balls. Afterward, he turned things up a notch. He hit balls in the gaps, high choppers, line drives, you name it.

A hard-hit ball can cover the eighty-four feet from home to second base in a fraction of a second. Even when I knew a ball was out of my reach, I dove for it, hoping Coach Adam would acknowledge the effort.

I struggled a bit executing double plays and got a lot of tough throws. Infielders use smaller gloves because they have to react fast and get the ball back out again. Ever since I was little, I have used my big sister's glove, and I've gotten so comfortable with a large glove that it kind of stuck with me. Using a small glove just never felt right. That's unfortunate for me because I had a hard time finding the ball in my glove. I'm also used to leveraging my body when I pitch, so I felt off-balance and strained to throw balls accurately to first base.

I think I redeemed myself, however, by making some great catches in shallow outfield—that space between the infielders and outfielders. I was able to get a positive read on hits and some good first steps to get to them. I even saw Coach Adam pause to give me a slight nod. With that look of approval, I attacked the ball more aggressively, play after play. I hoped he gave me extra credit for effort.

By the time Coach called us back in for a water break, I was covered with grass stains and sweat.

"Dude. It looks like you tie-dyed your uniform!" Teresa laughed.

If I'd caught more balls out on the field, I would've been wearing the grass and dirt with pride. But since all I'd managed to do was dive and *miss* most of the balls, the stains were more like a mark of shame.

Maybe I really wasn't good enough.

No. I stopped myself mid-thought. That kind of negativity wasn't going to get me anywhere. I felt Ellie telepathically sending me good vibes. I was too good—and had practiced too hard—to let a couple missed balls throw me off my game. Then one of my favorite Dadisms crept inside my head.

I hoped I sounded more confident than I actually was as I told Teresa:

"A LITTLE DIRT NEVER HURT."

"Ha. I like that," Teresa said. "A little dirt never hurt."

I told her it's what my dad always says.

"Cool," Teresa nodded. "Super cool."

When Coach Adam assigned everyone to new positions, he put me in a group with Kristy and Olivia in center field. I recognized Olivia from the cheers earlier in the day and from her snatching a couple hits off my pitches. I sprinted out with an extra skip in my step. I was fired up. When I got out to the grass, I heard footsteps behind me.

Kristy: "You're the little Garcia, right? Ellie's sister."

Me: "Yes, well, I'm Ellie's sister, but I'm not, you know, I'm not *little*—"

Kristy gave me a smile. "It's nice to officially meet you."

Kristy was being so nice I didn't want to correct her and tell her that we'd actually met many times before, after a few of their travel tournaments and also at the team's year-end party two years ago.

"Wow. Little Garcia," Kristy said again with a laugh. Olivia snickered with her. I started to feel like maybe Kristy's and Olivia's attitude wasn't niceness after all. Maybe they were teasing me.

I also thought maybe this competitive mentality Coach Adam worked so hard to foster turned these girls into *mean* girls, not *team* girls. Not everyone was as hard-working and supportive as Ellie.

Kristy may not have remembered me, but I remembered Ellie's stories about her. "She's a super stud," Ellie had said. "A ball-hogging, softball-eating stud."

Kristy knew she was a great player, and that gave her an edge—in personality as well as on the field.

When Coach stepped up to home plate to hit balls to the outfield, Kristy looked at the prospective players like she was going to eat us for lunch. "You want to go first, Little?" she asked. Olivia laughed at Kristy's intentional mistake.

"Sorry," Kristy said quickly, "I mean, do you want to go, *Sophia*?"

"Sure," I said, trotting into place on the grass, leaving the other two off to the side to watch—and probably to judge. I wasn't going to get into it with Kristy, especially not with Coach Adam watching.

"Here we go!" Coach yelled as he smacked a fly ball off his bat. My body started to move before the ball was even hit. Dad calls that a positive first step. He says it takes players years to gain that instinctive reaction, and sometimes they never get it. My feet were flying under me, but my eyes were fixed on the target. I chased it, watching the bright yellow ball fly farther and farther back. The grass turned to dirt under my cleats. I, the clueless infielder, didn't think about it because I'm used to running on the infield dirt, but I *later* learned the warning track is a sign the outfield wall is quickly approaching. I kept running and put my glove up, **s-t-r-e-t-c-h-i-n-g** my arm as high as it could go, and before I knew it—

SMACK.

My body slammed against the wall, and I literally saw stars for a second as I slumped to the ground. I assessed my body to make sure everything was still intact, but a wave of embarrassment hit when I saw that the ball was not in my glove but sitting on the ground next to me. I tried to get to my feet quickly, but considering the hit I just took, I was slow-moving. To add insult to injury, Olivia and Kristy laughed at me. Like I didn't already feel bad enough.

"You all right?" Coach Adam yelled across the field. I put a thumb up so he could see and nodded.

I trotted back behind Olivia and Kristy, when all I *really* wanted to do was climb into a hole in the ground.

"Ouch," Olivia said, as if she needed to point out how much worse it looked than it felt.

I tried to avoid eye contact and ignore them altogether, but I could feel the blood rushing to my face. I grabbed a lace from my glove and started pulling on it to stop myself from hitting them, which is what I really wanted to do.

When another girl trying out moved into position for her turn in the outfield, Kristy couldn't help piping up. "Didn't you notice that warning track, Little?" she asked. "I mean, they call it a *warning* track for a reason."

I watched silently as other players caught balls hit to left and right fields. Their throws into the infield were measured and recorded. By the time Coach Adam called everyone in for a final cheer, the pecking order was well established.

From city to city

The Waves show no pity.

From state to state

We dominate.

From coast to coast

We are the most.

Go . . . Waves!

I went home with mixed feelings about playing for the Waves. All I could do was wait.

August 30 • THE ROSTER

Final Roster: Waves Travel Ball Team

Kristy Major/Captain	CF	Trinity Middle School
Sara Brooks	1B	Our Lady of Mercy
Kim Cheung	C	Trinity Middle School
Selena Mendoza	RF	Penfield
Marcia Simone	2B	Emmanuel Middle School
Tasha Brown	SS	Garden City
Olivia Jenkins	LF	Garden City
Madison Morency	OF	Harvard Middle School
Alexandra Morency	3B	Harvard Middle School
Monique Vargas	P	Moorpark Middle School
Leigh Larson	P	Mt. Carmel Middle School
Rosie Goldberg	IF	Penfield

Head Coach Adam Devine

The Waves' final roster, released on the Wednesday after tryouts, included the best twelve-year-old softball players in Ventura County.

The most dominant hitters and fielders.

The girls who will probably win the league championship.

But I wasn't on the roster! Neither was Teresa. Or Becky.

I was positive I'd make the team as a sub at least, even though that meant the only position I was guaranteed to play was benchwarmer. The whole backup thing was like a consolation prize, but I was willing to go with it just to be on the Waves. Just to follow in Ellie's footsteps.

At first, I thought it was some kind of oversight. I reread the email at least five times. But my name wasn't on the final list. It was no mistake.

Ellie had been the star of the team, so I assumed I would make the roster as well. I worked hard. I love softball as much as Ellie.

I'm still not sure what went wrong. ☹

September 1 • NOT MAKING WAVES

What do you do when your dreams are crushed? When your whole future is ripped away? Not making the Waves was pretty much the worst thing that's ever happened to me. Maybe I can plead with Coach Adam for another chance, wait for him after practice and explain how important playing for the team is to me. Maybe if I convey my commitment and desire, he'll change his mind.

I am *meant* to be on that team. It's my destiny.

Mom and Dad tried to tell me it wasn't the end of the world, but I'm not convinced.

"I know you're disappointed, cariña," Mom said, using a term of endearment to soften the blow. "But there's always next season."

"Ugh. Next season is, like, a million years away."

"Life has a tendency to throw curveballs," Dad said as he stroked his mustache. "But when the right pitch comes, you'll be ready to hit it out of the park."

Sometimes his baseball metaphors are just too much.

Mom offered up some valerian root to calm my nerves. She's

the queen of home remedies: honey lemon tea or mullein for a cold, chamomile to ease stomach pain, and aloe for everything else.

There was only one thing that could make me feel better, so I called my friend Casey. We've been besties since the first month of kindergarten when Mom took Ellie and me to the school playground and I saw a cute little blonde wearing ruby red slippers. I recognized her from class, but was too shy to say hello.

I kept staring at her and those slippers until Ellie said, "Do you know her, Soph?"

"Um, I think she's in my class."

"Well, go say hi to her."

"I don't know her name."

"Say hi anyway. I'll go with you."

I was nervous, but we walked over, and Ellie said, "Hello. Are you two in the same class?"

Casey giggled and looked nervously to the ground, putting a finger in her mouth. "I think so."

"Cool. What's your name?" Ellie asked.

"Casey."

"This is Sophia." Ellie shoved me in Casey's direction. Casey's mother smiled and let the introduction unfold. "So now that you two know each other, why don't you play together?" When we didn't say anything, Ellie hopped on one of the swings.

Finally I said, "I really like your red shoes. They're like Dorothy's. Do you like *The Wizard of Oz?*"

"Yes!" She looked up and took the finger she was chewing out of her mouth. "That's one of my favorite movies!"

"Mine too!"

From there, we grabbed each other's hand and joined Ellie on the swings. We had a contest who could swing the highest and kick the eucalyptus branches in front of us.

Casey's mom invited us to her house for a quick snack, and I had bagel chips for the first time. We set up future play dates, and that was the beginning of our friendship. From that point on, we made memory after memory of watching *The Wizard of Oz*, eating bagel chips, and camping out in her backyard.

"I'm so sorry, Soph," Casey said. "I know how important making that team was to you. Why don't you come over? We can camp out tonight!"

"Aw, hon!" Casey's mom squeezed me when I walked into their house an hour later. "I'm sorry to hear the news about softball. Maybe some snacks will help cheer you up?"

I walked over to the familiar kitchen table and plopped down in front of a bowl of bagel chips.

"Casey's upstairs gathering some stuff for your campout." Mrs. Gaines said. "Her uncle got some fun finger lights the last time we went up to the cabin."

"Oh, sweet!" I said as Casey tramped down the stairs with an armful of supplies.

We set up the tent in her backyard. As soon as it got dark, we crawled in. We've done this so many times, it's like a second home. We call the tent our "friendship fort." Casey's a lot like me—kind of a tomboy who's not afraid to get dirty, but also really shy with new people. Luckily, we have each other to help navigate new situations. Casey's an only child, so she loves having a "sister," and her backyard has been the scene for all kinds of worlds we imagined together, from the lands of Oz, to African safaris, to grown-up homes with new babies and busy kitchens.

We covered our heads with a blanket. When we put the LED finger lights, which were the size of pistachio nuts, in our noses and ears and on our fingers, we looked like aliens. It was even better because we made up our own language, which sounded like Wookiee talk.

As we got ready for bed, we took the tiny lights out of our ears and noses but kept them on our fingers to make a light show on the ceiling.

"Are you freaked out at all about middle school?" Casey asked.

"I guess. But we'll do what we've always done—not worry about everyone else."

"I don't know." Casey sounded unsure.

I put the mini lights back in my nose and said in my best Wookiee voice, "Dooon't waarry. We weeel always haav each odder!" as I gave her a big alien hug.

Spending the night at Casey's was exactly what I needed. It helped me forget the Waves and remember the amazing people in my life.

September 3 · QUAKES CALL

There is a Spanish word, *querencia*. It doesn't really have a direct English translation, but it means the place you feel most at home. Not necessarily a physical place, but a place where your heart lives. My querencia is a softball diamond or team dugout. And not having a place to call home this season feels nothing short of TRAGIC.

When I got home from Casey's, hanging on a hook in front of me was Ellie's Waves cap. I stomped into her bedroom and threw it on her bed. "Take it back!" I cried.

"Hold onto the cap," Ellie said. "And I'll practice with you so you can try out again next year."

"I'm done," I announced. "If I can't play for the Waves this season, I don't want to play at all."

I remember crying myself to sleep before my first day of third grade because Ellie was starting at Monte Vista Middle School and wouldn't be in elementary school with me anymore. Last month, she walked me around the MV campus so I could learn my way around before school started. She said it was scary getting used to a new schedule with different classrooms. Since she got lost on her first day, she didn't want the same thing to happen to me.

Worse than getting lost would be showing up at my new school knowing I didn't make the Waves.

So I developed a cough and complained of a sore throat and fever. I was dying, I tell you! Dying! The sudden illness didn't go over very well with Mom, who made it clear that skipping school was *not* an option.

I'm not sure if I'm more embarrassed or disappointed about not making the team, but whatever the emotion is, I don't like it. I really do feel sick. #LifeSucks

Softball has defined me for so long. If I'm not a softball player, who am I? Sure, I can try out for another sport—I'm pretty good at basketball, and I like running—but softball just fits me like a glove (pun intended). Plus, Ellie is a softball player, and I love sharing the game with her.

And then, just when I thought I'd have to hang up my cleats forever, the phone rang.

I saw Mom listen intently and then whisper something to Dad. They conferred briefly before handing the phone to me.

"Hi, Sophia," an unfamiliar voice said.

"Who's this?" I asked tentatively.

"It's Jane Bryant, Teresa's mom."

Awkward silence.

"The reason I'm calling is because we're starting up a new team and we'd like you to be part of it."

More silence.

"We're joining the California Quakes," she continued. "I'm starting a twelve-and-under team."

My first inclination was to pass. To be honest, at first I almost *passed out*!

"I'm . . . not sure," I said.

"I know you're disappointed about the Waves. But we could use another pitching arm, and I think you and Teresa can really make an impact. Plus, we'll have a lot of fun!"

"Thanks, Mrs. Bryant. But I need to talk to my parents," I said, hoping to buy some time.

"That's fine. And everyone calls me CJ," she said. "Short for Coach Jane. The only condition is that if you do commit to the Quakes, you have to commit one hundred percent," CJ continued. "You can't start practicing and playing and then decide you want out. If you play for the team, you have to promise to play the *whole* season. Even if the Waves come calling. Even if you're frustrated with the growing pains of a new team. Even if—well, there can't be any ifs. Either you're in or you're not. First practice is this Saturday at White Oak Park."

The call ended, and I was more confused than ever. Life was swirling around me so fast—new school, new teachers, new classmates, and now possibly a brand-new team. I chewed on a ragged fingernail as I considered all the changes.

Mom suggested I make a list of pros and cons.

PROS	CONS
Fresh start	Untested team
Chance to play this season	May suck
More playing time?	Don't know any of the players except Teresa
I like Teresa	If I hate it, I can't leave
I can work on my skills for Waves tryouts next year	Too much change at once
I can show the Waves what they're missing	It's not the Waves

September 4 • DECISION TIME

I tossed and turned all night going back and forth over the pros and cons on my list. The last time I looked at the clock, it was three in the morning.

Next thing I knew, Dad tossed a softball glove at me. "Get up! Let's go!" he shouted from the bedroom doorway.

"What? Where are we going?" I rubbed my eyes, trying to emerge from a deep sleep.

"Come on. Get dressed and meet me out front. Let's throw."

I looked at my alarm clock, which I hadn't set. Less than five hours' sleep. I put my pillow over my face and yelled, "Come on, Dad! It's WAAAAY TOOOOO early."

After some procrastination, I rolled out of bed, got dressed, and grabbed my running shoes. But when I saw the blue laces, it reminded me of the Waves.

"Good morning, sweetheart," Mom called from the kitchen. "I have some chorizo burritos for breakfast when you're done."

I paused in the hallway, closed my eyes, and inhaled the aroma, drifting into a dream state.

Mom threw a pot holder at me. "Better get moving! Dad's waiting out front for you."

Struggling to keep my eyes open, I navigated my way to the bathroom. When I finally opened my eyes fully and caught a glimpse of myself in the mirror, my hair was crazy! I looked like I was straight out of a horror film—like I had been lost in the wilderness for days.

I pulled an elastic hair tie out and attempted to tame my crazy curls, but there were too many wayward strands that weren't long enough to make it into my messy bun. My instinct was to return to my room and put a cap on, but then I remembered—the Waves cap. I stopped in my tracks and hung my head.

Outside, Dad was talking to our next-door neighbor, who was walking his Labrador, Libby. Dad could be on the other side of the world surrounded by people who spoke a different language, but that wouldn't stop him from talking to everyone. He's such a friendly guy and a great storyteller. (Ninety percent of his stories aren't true, according to his sister, my Aunt Eileen. But that doesn't matter—he's so entertaining.)

"Hi, Mr. Martinez," I muttered as I stumbled over, still suffering from sleep deprivation.

"Good morning, Sophia. I see your dad has you up and working hard this morning. What dedication."

I smiled and nodded. *Yeah, not by choice!*

"It's about time you made it out here," Dad said to me as Mr. Martinez tugged Libby's leash and walked off.

"All right, Dad. I'm up, even though it's practically dawn on MY LAST DAY OF SUMMER VACATION!"

"Early bird gets the worm."

"Who said I wanted worms?" I mumbled.

I was walking out to the spot I normally pitch from when he stopped me.

"Where're you going? Over here on the grass. Start with your spins. Do it right."

I stopped in my tracks, threw my head down with another big sigh, and turned to the little strip of grass between the sidewalk and the street. I took a knee and began working my spins. The

Changeup grip   Fastball grip

biggest difference between a fastball, a curveball, and a screwball is the direction the ball spins and its rate of spin, so it's important to perfect that. Dad sat on a giant bucket with a padded lid and caught for me.

We threw back and forth in silence for a bit.

Finally he asked, "How did you sleep last night?"

"Not great. I couldn't get that pro/con list Mom told me to put together out of my head."

"Well, what did you come up with?"

"The lists are equal. There are just so many unknowns with the Quakes." I shuffled back a step to try a curveball. "With the

Waves, I knew what to expect. I watched every one of Ellie's games. I thought I'd follow right in her footsteps. I mean, what did she have at my age that I don't? What am I missing?"

"It's not about what Ellie had that you don't. Each team goes through phases of what they need and what they don't need. They needed a few position players, but they were set with their pitching staff. When Ellie tried out, they had just lost their ace pitcher. The timing was right."

I took a little longer with the next pitch as I pondered Dad's words. He had a good point. "But what if I hate the Quakes? What if no one likes me? What if they're awful? According to CJ, I can't just quit the team. What if I'm stuck?"

Dad caught the next pitch and held the ball. "Sophia Maria Garcia, *quitting* is not a word in our vocabulary. Mija, when we give our word, we keep it. That's not a CJ thing, that's not a softball thing, that's a Garcia thing."

When Dad finally threw the ball back, he instructed me to work my curveball spin. A few more pitches came and went as I considered his next words.

"Growing up can be scary. There are so many unknowns. And no guarantees in life. Sometimes we take risks and we lose big-time. Other times, it's the biggest risks that have the most payoff." He corrected my grip, then continued. "I was recruited by colleges when I was in high school, and I was scared. No one in my family had ever gone to college, and my fear of the unknown got the best of me. I always think back on that and wonder, *what if*? Don't *ever* let fear hold you back."

"Well, it's just one season," I said. "I mean, it's not like I have to sign my life away or anything." My heart leapt with the decision. "Okay. I'll do it!" Just knowing that I would be getting back on the field revived my enthusiasm.

Right on cue, we heard salsa music coming from the house. That was Mom's way of getting our attention for breakfast. If it weren't for Mom, we'd starve to death practicing.

Ellie joined us as we floated into the kitchen, following the scent of huevos rancheros, our favorite breakfast dish. In the kitchen, Mom was at the sink dancing. Ellie and I linked arms and mimicked Mom, swinging our hips. Dad worked his way over and grabbed Mom's hands, and they cut loose like they did in high school. They were so in rhythm, the way he spun her around and dipped her and then back up again and side to side. Ellie and I tried to do the same, but when I dipped Ellie, I almost threw my back out.

My family provides the rhythm for my life. They are my heartbeat. I don't usually notice because it's so constant. But there are moments like this, when the music is so loud, it feels like we'll never stop dancing.

September 5 • FIRST DAY OF MIDDLE SCHOOL

I can't write much because I'm still processing everything that happened today. The good news: Casey is in my math class, and I have English with my cousin Christina. Other than that, the day was just a whirlwind. There were lots of assessments and introductions and lectures on expectations. The fact that everyone was nervous made everything awkward, especially in classes where I didn't know anyone. On a scary scale of one to ten, today was at least an eleven.

Learning how to open my locker was way easier than I thought it would be, but learning my way around was much harder. I'm so glad Ellie already gave me a tour of the school because I would have gotten lost even more often than I did.

Sixth graders have lunch fourth period, and the lunch area, beneath a large overhang in the yard, is where everyone gathers. I brought a PB&J sandwich from home, but lots of kids stood in the cafeteria line and filled their trays with a hot meal.

The bell schedule is still confusing, but Ellie promises it will get easier. For now, I just need to keep straight which books to bring to which class and not lose the new school supplies Mom bought me.

September 9 • PRACTICE

Three Things You Control Every Day

1. Effort
2. Attitude
3. Actions to be a great teammate

(Team handout)

Glad to have the first short week of school over because today was our first official Quakes practice. The first thing I saw was the roster hanging on the fence—notice my name at #2!

1.	Michelle Rafa	Right Field
2.	Sophia Garcia	Infield/Pitcher
3.	Destiny Clinton	Catcher
4.	Lauren Rosen	Center Field
5.	Charlotte Martin	First Base
6.	Zoe Evans	Shortstop
7.	Julie Siegel	Outfield
8.	Yolanda Hall	Left Field
9.	Becky Compton	Second Base/Infield
10.	Kendall Carson	Third Base/Catcher
11.	Lillian Berube	Infield
12.	Teresa Bryant	Pitcher

Head Coach Jane Bryant

This time, I knew the drill. Before Dad and I parted ways, he grabbed my arm and said, "Pump the umph!" Then, "Remember, you deserve to be here, so act like it! You got this, kiddo!"

I smiled and headed hesitantly to the dugout while he set up his chair down the line. He brought a newspaper with him, but I knew he wouldn't be able to read it. He was going to keep an eagle eye on me throughout practice.

As I hooked my bat bag on the fence, I heard other girls greet one another. A lot of them had played together on CJ's rec teams over the years. Teresa knew almost everyone and was chatting with Julie, a girl I recognized from school. I averted my eyes, hoping no one would want to initiate a conversation. For now, at least, I would stay on the social sidelines.

When Teresa spotted me, she ran over and gave me a big hug. "I'm so glad you're on the team." She beamed. "So, so glad."

Teresa continued her rapid-fire chatter as she pulled me over to the bull pen. She asked me a bunch of questions, especially about Ellie, who she's seen pitch before. It seems like anyone who has anything to do with softball around here has seen Ellie play. And then my thoughts betrayed me: *Great, another Ellie fan.* It's not that I'm jealous of Ellie, but sometimes I get tired of being compared to her and usually coming up short.

We finished working on our pitch spins and moved to the mound. I knew Teresa was good from the Waves tryouts, but today I discovered just *how* good she really is. She not only has all the same pitches that I have, but she throws harder than I do. And . . . she has a rise ball. The backspin on a rise ball makes hitters think it's rising as it moves toward them. Then they try to hit it—and miss.

Most twelve-year-old pitchers don't have a strong enough rise ball to actually throw in a game. If a rise ball doesn't move enough, it's just a big, fat, high fastball left out there for hitters to crush. I mostly focus on getting my other pitches to move, so I haven't even tried to throw a rise ball.

Based on that, I don't see myself pitching much this season. Not because Teresa is the coach's daughter or favoritism, but because she's good. *Really* good.

CJ's affable features were framed by short-cropped dark hair. She has a gentle wisdom and attempted to form a bond with us right away.

"Know why Cinderella was kicked off her softball team?"

"Why?" we asked in unison.

"She ran away from the ball."

A few groans.

"Anyone know why Cinderella was bad at softball?" she continued.

We shook our heads.

"She had a pumpkin for a coach." CJ mimed a rim shot to take her joke over the top. "Seriously, this is my first time coaching a travel team, so I'm gonna need all the support I can get. When I played at Stanford, we had a commitment to excellence in all aspects of our lives. Hopefully I can coach better than a pumpkin!" She laughed.

There are a few players, including Teresa, Lauren in center field, Becky at second, and Destiny as catcher, who already showed excellence on the field. Lauren, in particular, surprised me on every play with her speed and incredibly strong throwing arm. Plus, her love of the game is contagious. Looking at where everyone else plays, I'm still not sure where I fit in.

Before going home, CJ passed out a bunch of official paperwork, including a league Code of Conduct that says any coach or player affiliated with the team who violates the following rules will be suspended or disqualified:

- *Unsportsmanlike conduct or derogatory action on or off the playing field*
- *Playing under an assumed name or falsifying an official document*
- *Recruiting or poaching active players during the regular season or postseason*

I'm pretty much a rule follower, and I love playing too much to start trouble, so there's no way I'm breaking any rules. I folded up the papers and tucked them neatly in my bat bag.

September 11 · BACK IN THE SADDLE

Monday morning, Casey ran up to me right when I got to school.

"Where were you this weekend? I called at least ten times. I was hoping we could go to the mall to look at these super cute jeans."

When I told Casey I had practice, she seemed disappointed.

"But I thought you said you weren't going to play. Or you didn't make the team or whatever?"

"Yeah, I know. But this other team ended up asking me to play, so that's where I was. With school starting and so much happening, I forgot to tell you!" I was going to share details, but I could tell Casey didn't really want to hear more. She's used to softball being a big part of my life. Every once in a while, she'd even go to the elementary school with us to shag balls. She's never showed any desire to play on a team, which is probably a good thing since she's not that great, but she still loves to be out there, like she's part of the family too. But lately I've noticed that Casey seems a little annoyed by the amount of time we dedicate to softball. And travel ball now takes us away more weekends than not, which means fewer campouts at her house.

"I'm so sorry, Casey. I promise I'll make it up to you. How about we go to the mall tomorrow after school?"

That sparked her interest. "Okay, yeah! That sounds great!" she shouted, splitting down a different hallway to her next class.

I was happy to salvage that conversation. Balancing school, softball, homework, family, and friends can be hard. Casey must feel like she's last on the list sometimes. We've been best friends since we bonded over our fear of flying monkeys—I didn't want to let her down.

In math class, I scrambled to finish my ratios and exponents worksheet because Ellie promised she'd work with me on my pitching after school. And now that I had plans tomorrow with Casey, I needed to stay ahead of my homework. That's something our parents won't cut us *any* slack on. Schoolwork always comes first. They say that playing sports is a privilege, and if we can't keep up with school, we have to stop playing softball. Well, *that* isn't an option, so we have no choice other than to do well in school!

I got home and ran to Ellie's room to find her focused on a biology assignment.

"Ellie, come on! You promised!" I shouted as I changed out of my school clothes.

"I know, I know. Ten minutes, I swear. I just have to finish these cell diagrams for biology class," she called.

I ran through the empty house and into the garage to grab my glove. Dad usually works late and Mom is a cashier at the local grocery store, so they leave it up to Ellie and me to take care of ourselves after school. We're pretty good at making quesadillas with flour tortillas and melted cheese. If we're lucky, there is some leftover carne asada or chicken in the fridge, and we make sliced beef or chicken quesadillas.

While I waited for Ellie in the garage, I whipped my pitching arm around, popping the ball into my glove. That sound always makes me feel so powerful. *Pop! Pop!* The acoustics of the garage exaggerated it a little too.

"Careful, or you'll rip a seam in your glove," Ellie pointed out as she hopped down the step into the garage.

"*Finally.*" My tone was full of annoyance, but I was actually excited to see her. "So what can you show me about rise balls?"

"Rise balls! Are you sure you're ready?" Ellie not only has a good rise ball, she has two. One is a typical rise ball that tempts hitters *just* enough before it rises above their bat and out of the strike zone. Her other rise ball is the deadliest, though—a low rise.

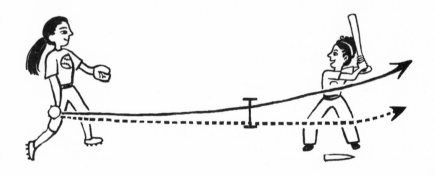

These are *so* hard for hitters to see. They start out low, and low pitches normally mean they'll move left, right, or down—not up. Her low rise starts below the strike zone, and hitters normally lay off it, thinking it will be a ball, but then it rises up into the strike zone, completely catching them off guard.

"The first thing I can tell you about a rise ball is that it doesn't start with the ball." Ellie took it from my hands.

"What do you mean?" I asked, completely confused.

"It starts with strength. Look at these puny little legs!" She grabbed my thighs. "If you want to be a rise ball pitcher, you need to do some strength training. Most of your power is in your legs, so that's where we start."

Back when Ellie really got serious about softball, Dad and Ellie transformed the garage into a makeshift gym. She walked to a corner and grabbed what looked to be an old broom handle with two jugs of water tied to each end.

"Like this," she said, demonstrating. She put the broomstick onto her shoulders behind her neck. Then she stood with her legs shoulder-width apart and said, "Time for squats." She crouched like she was going to sit on a chair, then stood up again. Then she switched her feet up and did lunges, stepping forward left, then right, with the weight still on her shoulders.

Next, she put the contraption down and moved an old wooden box on its side, stepping up with one foot and back down. "Do three sets of ten. Squats first, then lunges, then box lifts. Get those thighs burning! And especially build up your quad and glute muscles." She walked over to an old boom box and punched PLAY. The driving beat of her workout soundtrack filled the garage.

"This was not the afternoon I had in mind," I yelled over the music.

"Aw, come on. I'll do the exercises with you. Unless you don't care about getting stronger. In that case, you can just go and mope about not playing," Ellie said with a smirk.

"Okay, okay." It was kind of fun rotating stations with my sister and singing horribly to each song on her playlist.

September 12 • THE MALL

After school, I was waiting for Casey by my locker when my cousin Christina approached with some friends. They all had dark gelled hair pulled back in perfect high ponytails. This is the first year Christina and I have gone to school together. She just moved from across town and is now in my school district.

"¿Cómo estás, chica?" Christina greeted me.

"I'm good. How are you guys?" I couldn't stop looking

at Christina's thick eyelashes, which she expertly curled with a teaspoon.

"We're walking over to the skate park to hang out. Wanna come?"

Just then, I spotted Casey hurrying across the quad. "Um, I actually have plans with Casey. I promised her I'd go to the mall today."

"The mall? Since when do *you* shop at the mall?" Christina chortled.

My cheeks warmed. In our family, we mostly get hand-me-downs from cousins or siblings. We rarely get new clothes and when we do, it's from one of the discount stores like Walmart or Ross. Definitely not the mall.

"Casey saw some jeans she wants, so I'm going for moral support," I said.

As Casey approached, Christina and her friends looked her up and down. Christina has never approved of my friendship with Casey. All she sees is a blonde white girl in a trendy Gap shirt and brand-new pair of Vans. Definitely not our style—Hispanic style . . . at least according to Christina. Their whispers and smirks told me that much.

I wasn't really sure what to do or say, so instead of letting silence make things more awkward, I decided to evacuate.

Grabbing Casey's arm, I explained to Christina, "Sorry I can't make it today. Maybe next time." My cousin rolled her eyes and sucked in her breath. I could tell she took my response as a personal snub.

"What was that all about?" Casey asked as we walked away.

"Oh, nothing. Christina's disappointed I can't go to the skate park with her, that's all."

"You can go if you want."

"No, I want to check out those awesome jeans with you." I gave her a squeeze.

As we hit the parking lot, Casey steered me toward a group of girls who looked like they all belonged to the same country club. In fact, they all came from Aragon Elementary (coincidentally, right next to the Riviera Country Club), and Tiffany was more or less the group leader. They looked like clones, with the same hair color, makeup, outfits, everything.

What caught me a little off guard as we walked over was Casey. Really looking at her, I realized she could be one of them. I wondered if she *wanted* to be one of them.

"Hey, Tiffany! Hey, girls!" Casey called out.

"Hey," they all responded in a chorus.

"Sophia and I are heading to the mall. You want to come?"

I couldn't help but think: First, this was supposed to be a her and me outing, so why invite girls we barely know? Second, Casey may have more money than me, but it's not like she regularly shops at the mall. Was she trying to impress them?

"I wish," Tiffany said. "My tennis instructor is coming over after school. Maybe another time."

"Yeah, maybe another time. Good luck with tennis. See you later!" They all smiled and waved good-bye.

"Um, what was that?" I asked when we were out of earshot, still in shock from what I'd just witnessed.

"What was what?"

"Since when are you friends with Tiffany and her little clique?"

"I'm not sure I would call us totally *friends*. She's in my history class, and we've been talking. She's really nice. You would like her."

"Well, okay. It's just weird. Anyway, I'm happy they're not coming because I've been looking forward to just you and me time."

Casey's mom dropped us off at the Galleria Mall. On the ride, I couldn't help but worry about the new dynamics at school. My cousin Christina and I have always been close. We're almost the same age, but sometimes she treats me like a younger sister. The disappointment and judgment in her eyes were *heavy* when I turned her down. All of her friends are Hispanic, and don't approve of Casey, or don't like me doing "white girl" things like going to the mall. It seems like everyone is staking out their social space this year, and there's not a lot of room for overlap.

It scares me to see Casey trying so hard to be "in" with the cool kids. We've never cared about making an impression with anyone before, and now it seems that's all that's happening. We haven't even been in middle school a month, and already it's stressing me out.

When we got to the mall, Casey booked it to the department store to try on the coveted jeans. A series of annoying questions ensued. "Do you think they make my butt look too small? Do you think they make my legs look too short? Do you think they make my belly look like I have a muffin top?"

Casey didn't care about body image before, but now *everything* that came out of her mouth started with "Do you think?" I wanted to say back, "Why do you care what other people think? Do *you* like the jeans?!" But no, I was the supportive friend she needed today to assure her that everything made her look perfect. I missed the days of shorts and T-shirts and dirty bare feet from our backyard adventures. Now it was all about what's trendy.

We were at the mall for nearly two hours before Casey finally settled on a pair of jeans. Starving after all the changing room activity, we were headed to the food court when Casey grabbed my arm, her nails almost breaking my skin.

"Ouch!" I screamed.

"Shhh! Don't look! Oh. My. Gah! Just act normal. Oh, he's so hot. Act cool. I mean just act normal, but cool."

"What is wrong with you, Casey? You sound like a crazy person!" I scanned the area to process what she was freaking out about, but she kept yelling at me to not look *and* not look awkward. I'm pretty sure that is physically impossible. The only option I had was a crooked half-smile while looking wide-eyed at Casey. I'm pretty sure that is as uncool as a person can possibly look.

Finally, after what seemed like five horribly awkward minutes, but was probably only five seconds, Casey whispered, "Jason Brooks."

"Who?" I responded.

"You know, Jason Brooks, from math. He's *so* hot. I think we should go talk to him."

"What! No! You know I hate talking to boys. I always say the wrong things. I'll blow your cool-person cover." Who was this new Casey? When we met she was a shy girl in pigtails, and now she is the girl dragging me to talk to a *boy*!

"Oh, come on. Don't be such a baby." She dragged me over to Jason and a guy who looked like his older brother. I nibbled nervously on my thumbnail and kept the awkward half-smile pasted on my face.

"Hey, Jason," Casey said calmly—and quite flirtatiously, I might add.

"Oh, hey, Casey." Jason didn't look a whole lot less awkward or shy, which should have been a comfort, but just made me even more nervous.

"You know Sophia, right? She's in our math class too."

"Oh, right, right." He clearly didn't recognize me.

Casey nudged me to say something, but all I could bring myself to do was make my awkward smile a bigger awkward smile.

"So what are you guys doing here?" she thankfully interjected.

"My brother needed a new cap, and we thought we'd grab something to eat before heading home to face whatever awful thing our mom is making for dinner."

The way Casey laughed and flipped her hair was so impressive. It even made Jason blush a little. She was really good at this flirting thing.

"Yeah, I know what you mean. Well, anyway, we'll see you tomorrow, Jason. Good luck with dinner," she added with a cute giggle.

What was she talking about? Her mom's an *amazing* cook. I totally didn't get what was going on. It was like Casey was trying on a fresh personality with each new person she encountered.

"Yeah, okay. See you later, Casey."

"I think that went well," Casey said once we were in line for a pizza slice. "Do you think that went well? Did I sound okay? Do I look okay? I wish I was wearing my other red shirt and maybe a skirt."

"Casey, you were fine. Why do you care so much? I mean, he's just a boy. Those were just girls at school. I have never seen you try so hard or doubt yourself so much."

"Oh, Sophia, you don't get it. We're not in grade school anymore. It's all about first impressions. If you don't make a good first impression, you'll be forgotten. Don't you want to be popular?"

"Have I ever cared about being popular?"

"What am I going to do with you?" She laughed, wrapping her arm around me and kissing me on the forehead.

I know Casey was just trying to comfort me, but is this what middle school is all about? Focusing so much on what other people think? Do I have a cute enough body? Big enough here, but small enough there? Trendy clothes? Flirtatious giggle? Enough friends . . . enough of the *right* friends? It's too much to wrap my brain around.

Casey may have left the mall with an expensive pair of jeans I'm sure Tiffany would approve of, but I left with a dull ache in the pit of my stomach.

September 19 • IDENTITY CRISIS

Monte Vista Middle School has been a shock to my system on multiple levels.

I'm still trying to figure out the new ground rules. The biggest change, besides the size of the school, is all the kids coming from different neighborhoods. Blonde, brunette, white, African American, Asian, Hispanic. Our elementary school was pretty much all the same—mostly first- and second-generation Mexicans or Guatemalans. White kids like Casey were definitely the minority. But at the same time, we never cared about the differences. Now, the brown kids are the minority, and all of a sudden, people are starting to pay attention to skin and hair and eye color.

I'd never given much thought to my background, but today our English teacher, Ms. Resnick, assigned a story by Sandra Cisneros that changed that. She instructed us to break into small groups to analyze the writing together.

Once she gave the signal to get into groups, the class turned into a frenzy. Everyone tried to get with friends to avoid being the person left out. I scanned the room and saw my cousin Christina joining one group while Julie, my new Quakes teammate, joined another. In that moment, both Christina and Julie made eye contact with me and gestured for me to join their groups. I froze, reminded of when Christina wanted me to join her at the skate park.

My eyes darted back and forth between the two of them until finally Julie pulled me into her group. I took a seat, relieved that it was decided for me. I glanced in Christina's direction and shrugged, giving her a nonverbal *sorry*. She radiated the same disappointment I got the other day.

Ms. Resnick distributed Sandra Cisneros's novel *The House on Mango Street*, about a Latina girl growing up in a Chicago barrio. We took turns reading the chapter "My Name," featuring a girl named Esperanza who was ashamed of her Spanish-sounding name and her family.

Once we were done reading, there was a series of questions. The first: "What do you think Esperanza meant when referring to her great-grandmother, 'I have inherited her name, but I don't want to inherit her place by the window'?"

Everyone in the group turned to me.

"What?" I asked. "Why are you all looking at me?"

"Well, you know, because you're like Esperanza," said Matt, one of the boys who ruled the handball court at recess.

"*How* am I like Esperanza?" I returned his gaze. I knew what he meant, but I wanted him to say it out loud.

"Well, aren't you, like, Spanish or something?" Matt asked. Emily, the rosy-cheeked girl sitting next to him, giggled under her breath. He had been flirting with her since the first day of school.

Great, trying to be cool and flirt with a girl at my expense. My blood was boiling, but I was tongue-tied. I studied his face and slowly exhaled. "I don't know what it means." I had a lot of ideas about what it meant. I think it meant that Esperanza didn't want

to share the same sad story as her great-grandmother. She didn't want to be controlled by a man, not allowed to travel and dream as she pleased. She didn't want to be stuck looking out the window, wondering what could have been.

But I didn't say any of that because for the first time, my peers were judging me not simply as Sophia, but as Sophia *Garcia*. All of a sudden, they wanted "the Mexican's" perspective, not my perspective. I'm not ashamed to be Mexican, but it was the first time I was singled out by my peers as one.

I slid down in my seat and crossed my arms. I even caught myself clicking my heels together. Like Dorothy, I wished doing so would transport me home.

I glanced over at Christina's group, which was having a lively discussion. There were lots of smiles and laughter. I wished I had joined that group.

September 23–24: FALL BALL TOURNEY #1

This weekend was the Quakes' first softball tournament. I couldn't wait to escape the social boxes at school and get into the box in which I felt most at home: the batter's box. I'd been working hard with Ellie on my pitching, hitting, and strength training, and was super excited to play in a real game.

Dad had weekend shifts at work, and Mom took Ellie to her games, so I rode with CJ and Teresa. The Bryants even invited me to stay with them the *whole* weekend to make getting to the games easier. I couldn't believe it when CJ drove up in a brand-new BMW. Teresa rode shotgun, and I sat in the luxurious back seat and tried to keep from touching all the fancy volume and temperature controls.

In the dugout, CJ handed out our new green-and-gold jerseys. Mine had my name and number on the back: *Garcia, #25*. I couldn't wait to put it on.

I'm not sure what I expected during the first Quakes game, but it wasn't spending most of it sitting on the bench. I would have been okay as a benchwarmer for the Waves, but assumed (incorrectly) I'd be part of the Quakes' starting lineup, somewhere on the infield. Fortunately, substitution rules are flexible, and CJ put me in twice to pinch-hit.

My first at bat against the Dirt Dawgs, I was just excited to be hitting. I had a plan, like Dad taught me, and was looking for a drop ball.

The hardest part of hitting is transferring energy from your legs to your hips and torso and letting the momentum feed the swing. Dad calls this "the load." When the pitcher threw a drop ball, I lifted my front leg to drive that energy to my backside and then launched it forward toward the ball. The timing worked out perfectly. I hit a hard grounder down the third baseline. Charged with adrenaline, I took off, but the third baseman made a great backhand play to throw me out at first. Ugh.

My second at bat, I waited patiently for a high pitch. When one came across the plate, I loaded my swing and hit a really hard, deep fly ball. It sailed up, up, up . . . and descended directly into the right fielder's glove. I *so* wanted to get on base, and maybe score, but for the second time today, I was up and out.

Most star pitchers—or "aces"—like Teresa pitch every game, even if there are three or four games in a day. Dad calls pitchers like that "bulldogs" because they're so tough and can work hard. Ellie is a bulldog for sure. I hope to be too, someday.

The real star of the game, though, was Lauren, our defensive MVP. She made so many grabs in center field, I lost count. She's the whole package: fast, coordinated, can track balls well, and has a strong arm. Plus, she's a great hitter. On my prior teams, there wasn't a lot of action in the outfield, but with the Dirt Dawgs smacking long balls back-to-back, there was a lot of excitement out there today.

Much more excitement than in the dugout, which can be a lonely place when your teammates are all out on the field. After each half inning, I organized all of the helmets and bats and put them in their proper place. Each helmet and bat I touched was a painful reminder of my position as a substitute player with Julie and Lilly. Although I was disappointed, we cheered on our team, drumming overturned ball buckets with softballs.

Bang, bang! Defense!

Bang, bang! Defense!

During a lull in activity, Julie brought up the episode in English class. "Matt was totally out of line the other day. I'm sorry. I should have said something."

I recalled the encounter and felt conflicted all over again.

"Thanks, Julie. Appreciate it."

"It was plain rude. He's so snooty. I can't believe how he acts sometimes."

Julie turned her attention back to the field, just as Yolanda chased down another fly ball. "Why does YoYo always start?" she snarked, jerking her chin toward left field. "She's not *that* good." Was she testing me? Maybe she thought we'd bonded and wanted to see if I would join in her teammate bashing.

Ellie and I have always been taught to be good sports, so I took the challenge. "I think she's pretty good. And you can't forget about her hitting. She had that clutch RBI last inning."

Without making eye contact, she said, "I guess you're right.

Just not sure why I'm even on the roster if I'm not gonna play."

I didn't want to enable this—I wanted to support my teammates. Lilly side-eyed Julie and looked down at her phone. "What are you doing?" I asked Lilly, looking over her shoulder.

She had pulled up a tracking app. "Marking where each batter hits the ball when they come up to the plate. That way, I can give CJ a heads-up if adjustments need to be made on the field."

"That's so cool," I said. I decided to help Teresa by tracking her pitches to figure out what was working and what wasn't. It helped pass the time on the bench, and I started seeing patterns to bring up next practice.

The Bryants have a really nice house in Westlake with a pool and a waterslide in the backyard. The living room is *massive*, with vaulted ceilings, and I think they have, like, three different family rooms and a "game" room for Teresa and her two younger sisters. The house even *smells* elegant.

We hung out in Teresa's color-coordinated bedroom, and I couldn't help noticing all the jewelry, nail polish, and different kinds of perfumes displayed on her dresser. The only thing I've ever done with my nails is bite them. We picked different colors and painted each other's nails as we talked about the team, our friends at school, and even boys. I shared the story of Casey and me at the mall and how awkward I was around Jason. I talked about how much "game" Casey had and how confused I was about this whole new world of boys. I tried to recreate the awkward smile from that day, and she thought that was hilarious. We laughed so hard, we both were in tears. Seriously, I almost peed my pants.

"I guess I don't really have a problem talking to boys. Well, actually I just don't really think about it too much," she said as our laughter simmered down. "My sisters and I always play with the boys on our street, and we've been such jocks, we always played with them at school during recess. I guess it just comes natural."

I could see what she was saying. Ellie and I would challenge boys on our street to a Wiffle ball game every once in a while, but I wasn't trying to have a conversation with any of them.

Sunday morning, on our way to the fields, we stopped at Starbucks to pick up caramel macchiato Frappuccinos. My family and I always drove by Starbucks but have never actually had enough extra money to buy a drink there. It was like slurping ice cream for breakfast.

We were both amped for the game, but once again, I wasn't part of the starting lineup.

"I know you want playing time, and I promise I'm going to work you into the lineup more," CJ said to me during an inning change. "Putting girls in position is a lot like solving a Rubik's Cube, and I'm still figuring things out." She smiled.

CJ's words lifted my mood. It was actually reassuring to hear that she didn't have everything decided. *And* I managed to get on base with a shot to the outfield when I was put in to pinch-hit. Mostly, I focused on the energy and enthusiasm of my teammates while avidly cheering them through runs and errors.

Despite me not playing much, the day flew by. The Quakes—the newest team in the league—won the doubleheader and our bracket. We celebrated like it was New Year's Eve. Lauren and Teresa led the triumphant cheer:

> *We're all for one (we're all for one)*
> *We're one for all (we're one for all)*
> *Together we stand (together we stand)*
> *Together we fall (together we fall)*

And in the end (and in the end)

We win them all (we win them all)!

Hard to believe I just had one of the best weekends of my life . . . sitting on the bench!

(Our logo!!)

October 6 · ABUELITA'S TAMALE PARTY

My abuelita passed away a few years ago, but to celebrate her birthday, we still have a big tamale party. It's an event I always look forward to. There's a lot of preparation, and the wonderful smells floating around my house torture me for days in advance. To get ready, we soak corn husks, prepare and mix the masa until it is the right texture, roast the chiles, and cook the pork. ¡Ay, Chihuahua! It makes me hungry just thinking about it.

A few hours before the party, I was hanging out near my locker with Casey when Christina approached with her chola-styled friends. The latest song from the Mexican girl group Ha*Ash was blaring from the headphones draped around her neck.

"Hey, Sophia! I can't wait for later!" Christina shouted knowingly.

"Me too! My mom has been cooking all week!"

"I know what you mean," she said, pulling me in close to

whisper. "I stole some roasted chiles for lunch today!" She laughed. "You better not tell!"

I smiled. "Your secret is safe with me."

As Christina walked away, Casey asked, "What's happening?"

"My abuelita's party. You remember? We get together and make tamales using her recipe. It's almost like she's still here."

"Oh, yeah. That's awesome."

"Do you want to come?" It occurred to me that even though I've been friends with Casey since kindergarten, something had always come up to prevent her from eating Abuelita's tamales—vacations, competing family holiday celebrations—and this could be her first time tasting my favorite special-occasion food.

"Really? Your family always has the best parties . . . and *fooood!*" She shook my shoulders, pleading.

"Have your people call my people, and I'll see what we can do." I breathed on my chewed fingernails and polished them on my shirt.

"Have I told you how beautiful you look today? Your wonderful choice of jean shorts and fabulous T-shirt! And your smile is just so—"

"Okay, okay. Flattery will get you everywhere."

"Oh, thank you, thank you." She gave me a big hug. "What time should I tell my mom?"

I had to giggle. There is no start time for a Garcia family party. People just show up when they want and leave when they want.

"Anytime is fine," I told her. "I bet there are people already there."

We got off the school bus and were walking past a row of neatly manicured yards when the sound of violins and guitars drifted down the street. Casey heard it too. "Ooh la la! Sounds like a fun party!" She tried to salsa dance and walk at the same time. Got to give the girl credit for trying.

"Yes! Mariachi music." I smiled and joined in the dancing. We grabbed each other's hands and waltzed our way to my front door. This was the Casey I love, not the Casey constantly worried about each move out of fear of judgment. I visualized my cousins Mario and Walt, who play in a professional mariachi group, driving the percussive rhythm.

"Someone's going to call the cops. You have a rager going on!" Casey laughed.

"I don't think it will be an issue," I giggled, especially since Walt is a cop.

As soon as the front door opened, we were bombarded with sensory overload. The traditional mariachi music my abuelita loved filled the house, along with a mixture of Spanish and English conversation. The aroma of meat and spices was hypnotizing. Casey paused at the threshold for a second and scanned the room, looking for familiar faces, as if there was an invisible plane she couldn't pass through. I grabbed her hand and pulled her in.

"¡Ay! Cochina! There you are!" Aunt Eileen called from behind us as she pinched our butts. She was wearing a cotton dress with

vibrant-colored flowers embroidered all over it. "Hello, Casey! It's so good to see you," she said with a welcoming smile.

"Hi, Aunt Eileen," I greeted her, with a warm hug and a kiss on the cheek. Casey put her hand out to shake but quickly pulled it back when she realized her mistake. She knew better with my family—there's no such thing as personal space.

My aunt grabbed Casey into a big bear hug. "¿Qué tal? Are you ready to work? Go wash your hands and meet me in the kitchen. Cochina!"

My aunt Eileen has always called me cochina (which means *pig* or *piglet*) for as long as I can remember because I've always been a messy eater and I love playing in the dirt. I guess things haven't changed. ☺

After we washed up, my aunt set out separate bowls of masa, corn husks, pork, and chicken, along with a pot for our finished product. The smells were more enticing with each passing moment.

"The sooner we finish," said Ellie, who joined us in the kitchen assembly line, "the sooner we can eat!" She must have read my mind, because all I could think about was how hungry I was.

"So what exactly am I supposed to do?" Casey asked, eyes wide with excitement.

"Start by preparing the masa." Mom swooped in with instructions. "Then grab a corn husk and spread it out in your hand like this." She demonstrated by spreading a spoonful of masa on the husk.

"Now take the meat and put some in the middle. Not too much, because the masa has to go all the way around and fit inside the corn husk. Then you fold it up, kind of like a burrito." Mom expertly folded one end and put it in the pot to steam.

It took Casey a few tries to figure out the portion sizes. At first, some tamales had too much masa and some had too much meat. But eventually she got the hang of it.

"I always wondered what these were," she said, holding a corn husk.

"Yup. Key to making the best tamales ever!" I said.

Christina appeared out of nowhere and asked, "You've never had a tamale before?"

"I've seen them, but never knew what they actually were," Casey answered honestly.

Christina's smug face revealed what she was thinking. Tamales have been the bricks and mortar of our family forever. So many memories made in the kitchen with Abuelita cooking tamales and sharing stories. It's hard to wrap my brain around the fact that not every family makes and eats traditional Mexican food.

But then I remembered having Sunday dinner with Casey's family and being unfamiliar with their menu. Her mom made a noodle dish with sugar and sour cream called kugel, and we had

How to
make
TAMALES

① Soak CORN HUSKS
for 2 hours.

② Spread MASA on each
CORN HUSK.
(Masa is made from
finely ground corn meal.)

③ Add cooked FILLING —
pork, beef, chicken,
or chiles and cheese.

④ Roll it up and tie.

⑤ Steam for 2 hours.

⑥ EAT!

matzo ball soup to start. It occurred to me how different our worlds are, which is surprising, considering we've been such good friends for so long.

For the first time, our differences were as striking as our similarities. And that worried me. That is, until the food was served. What could worry me with such an incredible assortment of sweet and savory tamales?

Casey is now a tamale fan. Her favorite was the chile-and-queso tamale, made with cheese and peppers. She even said she'd order one the next time she sees it on a restaurant menu.

"There's nothing like Abuelita's tamales," Mom chimed in. "Extra love in every ingredient."

Aunt Eileen was quick to add with a wink: "And a hint of ancient spices."

As I lay in a food coma later, I was struck by several thoughts from the day. Strains of music and chatter flowed from the backyard patio as my thoughts wandered.

I'm proud of everything that makes me a Garcia, but I'm not sure where I fit in. At home, I'm spunky, full of family pride and love; at school and softball I'm a kind, loyal friend and teammate. There's a sprinkling of everything that makes me stand apart, like a blend of spices. Mostly I want to be remembered for me, Sophia. Not because I follow someone else's lead, but because I forge my own path. Is there a box you can tick for that?

October 14 • HUNTINGTON BEACH TOURNEY

Today's games were at a beautiful tree-filled park near Huntington Beach. The fields were so close to the Pacific that we could feel the cool offshore breeze. It was a crisp fall day, and my mind was in a great place. With both my parents working weekend shifts, CJ graciously invited me to stay with them again.

Our shortstop, Zoe Evans, joined us on the drive down to Huntington Beach. Teresa's dad drove his new SUV, and there were screens behind the front seats so we could watch DVDs during the ride. First, we watched the movie *Selena*, based on my favorite Tejano singer. We kept rewatching the parts when Selena, played by JLo (Jennifer Lopez), performed onstage. Zoe put her hair in a side ponytail and took off one of her sandals to use as a microphone. She was a surprisingly good singer and incredibly confident.

"We should sing the national anthem to kick off the tournament." Zoe laughed. "And be introduced as Sophia y Los Dinos," she added, referencing Selena's singing group Selena y Los Dinos.

Seated in the front passenger seat, CJ turned to us. "Stick to your day jobs, girls—playing softball," she said with mock seriousness.

Here is the lineup and batting order for today's games:

#	Player	Position
13	Zoe	SS
11	Becky	2nd
3	Charlotte	1st
99	Destiny	C
5	Kendall	3rd
21	Lauren	CF
4	Michelle	RF
10	Yolanda	LF
7	Teresa	P
-	SUBS	-
9	Lilly	IF
25	Sophia	P
27	Julie	OF

Our first opponent was the Diamonds, a pretty decent team from Santa Monica. By the fourth inning, we were up 4–0 and feeling confident. Teresa was going strong, but CJ wanted me to warm up just in case. Even if the starting pitcher is doing well, it sometimes helps to mix things up.

The four-run lead must have been enough of a cushion, because CJ decided to give Teresa a break and put me in to pitch.

I was *so* excited to finally get on the mound. I'd been tracking pitches and hitters all game, which helped relieve my nerves, and I felt fully prepared to shut the Diamonds down.

"Ball's in, comin' down!" yelled the umpire. The ball popped around from player to player—first, short, third, second, then to me. The infield slowly closed in as my teammates huddled around me on the mound.

"All right, Sophia. Let's shut 'em down!" Destiny said with a wink before pulling her catcher's mask down over her face. The full mask, combined with her matching chest protector, made her look like a Power Ranger.

"We got your back," our third baseman, Kendall, added, tapping her glove between my shoulder blades.

Standing in a circle, everyone put their hands in and yelled, "Hold 'em!" We wouldn't let the Diamonds get any runs. Then we smacked gloves together and returned to our positions.

I turned to face home plate and closed my eyes. *Remember your routine*, I heard Dad say in my head.

The first batter was the Diamonds' number five hitter. Typically, the leadoff hitter consistently gets on base however they can. Dad calls these hitters table setters. They get things started for the rest of the team to feed off.

Number two hitters have softball smarts. They read the defense and know the best place to put the ball in order to move the base runners. They often sacrifice themselves to move teammates into scoring position.

The number three and four hitters are typically really good hitters that get extra base hits. They hit a lot of doubles, triples, and even home runs.

Back to the number five hitter: a mixture of leadoff hitter and fourth and fifth hitters. She needs to keep a rally going and find a way to get on base, or come up with a big hit to score the base runners. So I scoped out this hitter to get a read on what her plan might be. I couldn't see her face well beneath the batting helmet, but her stance projected an aura of confidence. I knew from tracking her she was a solid hitter, but she'd struggled with Teresa's outside pitches as well as her changeup.

My first pitch was outside, and she took it for a strike. A good start. Miss Confidence was looking for an inside pitch, but I wasn't about to pitch to her strength. *Let's go for a drop ball*, I thought. She laid off again, for a ball. She was hungry to hit a good one. *How about a changeup?*

CJ must have been thinking the same thing, because that was the next pitch she relayed to Destiny. *Keep it low and outside.* My pitch wasn't as outside as I wanted, but it was enough to make the hitter go for it with an off-balance swing. She hit a weak grounder to Becky at second, for the out.

Boy, did that feel good! First out! I could finally breathe easier. The muscles in my arms, neck, and back relaxed. In short order, we got two more outs. I kept the ball down and outside for a few more groundouts, and boom, the inning was over.

When I jogged back to the dugout, Teresa and CJ were the first to greet me.

"Nice work!" Teresa said with a high five.

"Awesome job. Way to know your hitters," CJ said with a proud smile.

I tried to keep my game face on like it was no big deal, but inside I was bursting with pride. It was so good to hear that reassurance.

I couldn't revel in the moment for too long, though, because now that I was in for Teresa, I was on deck to hit. I grabbed a helmet and a bat and stood in the on-deck circle, studying the pitcher. She had a big blue bow in her hair, which distracted me for a second, but I quickly refocused.

Blue Bow must have been the Diamonds' only pitcher, because she was sucking wind and clearly tired. After watching her all game, it was obvious her best pitch was her drop ball. I knew from experience that I needed to shift to the front of the box and hit the ball before it dropped.

First up for the Quakes was Yolanda, our left fielder and seventh hitter in the lineup. YoYo's thick black hair was visible beneath her helmet as she ground out to the shortstop. YoYo had stood toward the back of the box, so I hoped my front-of-the-box game plan would work.

I approached the plate, and my dugout cheered me on:

See that batter at the plate.

She's the best in all the state.

She has spirit, she has pride.

Too bad for you she's on our side.

My heart beat erratically as I stepped into the batter's box, one foot at a time, and positioned myself toward the front. As I focused, my teammates' voices faded away.

The first pitch was too low and too far outside, so I took it for a ball.

The next pitch floated in right down the middle. A successful hitter knows to let her legs power the swing. I loaded my body by shifting my weight back, and then used my hands to lead the barrel of my bat right to the ball. I hardly felt it when I made contact. Those are the best kind of hits, when you don't even feel the impact. That's when you know you've nailed it.

The line drive sailed over the second baseman's head and into the right-center gap. I took off toward first and picked up on CJ waving me on to second base. I put my head down and powered around the corner as fast as possible.

The shortstop covering second was positioned to catch the ball, so I kicked it into high gear and slid feetfirst into the bag using all the momentum I could muster.

As my far foot touched the base, I heard the ball smack the second baseman's mitt and felt her tag my chest.

Still on my side in the dirt, I looked anxiously up at the umpire. The moment seemed to stretch out indefinitely until he raised his arms to shoulder level, signaling I was safe.

Sweet! I stood up, stepped on the base, and clapped the dust off my hands. Through the cloud, I saw my teammates on the fence screaming and cheering for me. I was going to have a nasty black-and-blue mark on my thigh, but it was worth it. I immediately flashed on another Dadism and chuckled.

NO STAINS, NO GLORY
NO BRUISES, NO STORY

Our next batter was Zoe, a ball of energy who reminds me of the Energizer Bunny because of her nonstop motion. Besides being a great singer and Selena impersonator, she's also a great teammate. Zoe laid down a sacrifice bunt, which forced her out but moved me from second to third base.

Then Becky hit a single up the middle to score me. I crossed home plate in a blur for **my first run of the season!** Instinctively, I looked up to the stands for my parents and experienced a momentary letdown when I didn't spot them. The disappointment was quickly replaced by a flurry of high fives as I floated into our dugout.

Score: 5–0.

Charlotte Martin, the biggest and strongest girl on our team, unexpectedly struck out to end the inning. Charlotte is an intimidating player who wears her heart on her sleeve. She doesn't talk much, but as she jogged out to the field to play defense, Char looked more than a little disappointed.

And just like that, I was on the mound again. This time, I faced the top of the Diamonds' lineup. The first girl at bat was a lefty slapper—a player who's fast and able to hit the ball on the run by chopping it hard off the ground or poking it into an opening on the field. Since they're so fast, slappers can usually outrun their own hit. Most don't like inside pitches, so I thought I'd start low and inside. Slapper Girl surprised me by laying down a beautiful drag bunt for a base hit.

Even though things weren't going as smoothly as last inning, I was determined not to let the pressure get to me. The next hitter knocked the ball to the left side of the infield, and Zoe made a good play on it at shortstop to get her out at first. Slapper Girl, however, progressed to second base.

A girl with a shin guard walked up to the plate next. I always feel bad when I see those. Normally if a player has a shin guard on, it means they hit one too many balls off their shin and need protection. I didn't want a ball hit to the outfield, so I agreed with

Destiny's drop ball sign. Shin Guard Girl laid off of it. The next pitch called was a curveball outside. Shin Guard smacked the ball right back at me. Thanks to my large glove, I was able to snag it for the second out. I have to admit, the hard line drive made my heart pound, but it didn't shake me. I was ready to get the third and final out of the inning.

The next hitter had eye black smeared on her cheekbones and an intensity that caught me off guard. Her teammates looked for inside pitches, but this girl liked outside ones. I had to mix it up.

My first pitch was a screwball, which Eye Black sent sailing down the third baseline for a foul. It was a hard hit, and it took me a second to catch my breath. *¡Otra vez!* I heard Dad in my head. In other words, shake it off.

So she likes outside pitches but just nailed an inside one. What does she not hit?

Let's try a changeup, I decided. I was right. She almost fell over when she swung and missed.

Overconfident, I threw another changeup. Not a good idea.

This time Eye Black sat on it and sent it *sailing* into the left-center gap. Lauren accurately tracked the ball and dove for it, making an awesome catch to end the fifth inning. Thank goodness I had an amazing defense behind me.

Everyone congratulated Lauren when she jogged into the dugout—everyone but Julie, who has been in an increasingly foul mood after limited playing time. She's come into games to base-run a few times, but that's been it so far this season. Julie is a pretty good outfielder, but nothing like Lauren, who is taller and stronger and super-fast. Just because there are open places on the roster doesn't mean there are oper[...]ns. Julie and I were learning the hard way.

We ended [...] Diamonds 5–0, and I was happy about ho[...]roundouts as pitcher.

[...]lebrating, Lauren and h[...] mom said, had some ne[...]

"[...]vin," Lauren started out. And t[...] to continue. We couldn't imagin[...]

"Yo[...]ied, and we all echoed the sentiment.

"Thanks. But that makes it even tougher to tell you all this," Lauren sniffed. Her mom comforted her as she continued sobbing.

"We're moving," she finally blurted out. It was like a punch in the gut. "My dad got a new job in Michigan, and we're leaving right away." By now she was choking on her words.

Mrs. Rosen stepped in when Lauren could no longer talk. "It's been such a privilege being associated with this team. Lauren has loved playing with you all. But we want to get her enrolled in a new school as soon as possible, so today was Lauren's last game with the Quakes."

We engulfed Lauren with hugs until her sobs receded. Here

I was, worried about all of the changes happening in *my* life. I couldn't imagine just up and moving to a whole different state across the country in the middle of a school year.

I'm happy that her last game ended on a good note, but I can't imagine our defense without Lauren. We said our good-byes and promised to keep in touch.

Julie, spotting an opportunity in the lineup, showed a renewed sense of team spirit.

October 15 • A SWITCH

Ellie and Dad were excited I got the chance to pitch in a real game. They wanted to hear a play-by-play of every inning. I ended by sharing Lauren's big reveal.

"It's a blow for us," I explained. "Just when we're starting to gel as a team. I mean, Julie can play that position—she wants to play that position—but Lauren is *so* good. And she always gets on base. And she's so fast she can beat out ground balls!" I felt bad not giving Julie more credit, but I honestly wasn't sure she could rise to the occasion.

"All right, all right, you three! If dinner gets cold, you'll have to cook me meals for a whole week!" Mom yelled from the kitchen. We all knew better than to let her food get cold, so we hightailed it to the dinner table.

Once we were seated and happily slurping tortilla soup, Mom revisited the weekend. "I'm so sorry we missed watching you play

again," she began. "Was it okay staying over at the Bryants'? Did you thank them for their hospitality?"

"You should see their house!" I started. "It's amazing! Teresa has her own glam station in her room. I have never seen so many nail polish colors." I tried to recall every detail of her house.

"What do you talk about?" Ellie chimed in.

"Oh, uh, you know. Whatever. School, friends, shopping . . . boys." I tried to squeeze that in under the radar.

"Boys! What do you need to be talking about boys for? Don't they have cooties?" Dad interrupted.

"Dad, come on. I'm not five years old anymore." He was smiling, but the way he looked down at his plate, I think it made him sad I was growing up. "CJ said the next time I stay at their house, we can go shopping and get manicures and pedicures at the salon!"

"Oh, wow! That's nice of them," Mom said. "But they're already doing so much for you, and us, by letting you stay with them and drive you to games. They really don't need to do that."

I wanted to say, *Why not? They can take me if they want to!* But I know better than that. Money is a touchy subject in our house, so I just let it go. I'm sure Mom will forget about it by next weekend, anyway.

After dinner, we were zoning out to *Seinfeld* reruns on TV when Dad said, "You know, I've been thinking about your team and Lauren moving and what you said about Julie. Something I learned playing ball over the years is how beneficial being a utility player can be."

"What do you mean?" I asked.

"Think of the girls sitting on the bench. Most of them only play one position, so their best shot at getting an opportunity is if the starting girl can't play for some reason. A utility player, however, can fill in for *anyone* on the field. The chances of getting into the game go way up."

"What are you saying, Dad?"

"I know how much you love pitching, but how much of it is pitching, and how much is it just *playing* the game?"

"Of course I love playing, Dad. I love everything about the game."

"What if you played the outfield in Lauren's place?"

Me? An outfielder! Panic rushed through my body. My whole

world, or at least the world of softball, has always been in the infield. I'm Ellie's Mini-Me. I've worked so hard on my pitching. Would all the work go to waste?

Dad must have read my thoughts. He put his hands on my shoulders. "Look, you're a good pitcher. I'm not saying you should give up on that. You can still work on your pitching, but in the meantime, what do you think about asking CJ to let you practice the outfield? See how it feels. Wouldn't it be worth giving it a shot to be able to play more?"

Even though I'd had a good run on the mound today, Teresa *was* the starting pitcher—my playing time would always be limited. I looked over at Ellie.

This would change everything. First not playing for the Waves, and now not pitching! What else can I fail at?

Ellie must have seen the tears forming in my eyes, because she moved from the far end of the couch and draped her arms around my neck.

"Sophia, you deserve to be out on that field. You're one of the better hitters on the team, and like Dad always says, if you're hitting well, they'll always find a spot for you in the lineup. That's hard to do when you only play one position and there's a stronger girl also playing that position. Think of this as an opportunity, not something you're settling for."

"Outfield is where they put the players who aren't good enough to play anywhere else." I sniffed. I know it's kind of a smug and annoying way to look at the situation, but that's how I felt.

"Did you watch the Women's College World Series? It's the outfielders that make the game-saving plays. It's always an outfielder robbing a home run that you see on *Sports Center*."

As usual, Ellie drilled right down to the truth. I don't always like her advice, but her support made me feel better. Deep down, though, I wondered whether we'd still get to pitch together. Would we still be as close?

"I know this is a lot to process right now, Sophia," Dad said, rubbing my shoulders. "I just thought I'd suggest it, and you can sleep on it."

But when it was time to sleep, my thoughts circled back to what Dad said—the idea that playing multiple positions can make a player much more valuable. I really do miss that energy and excitement of being on the field. I need to figure out if I have the courage to try something new.

What keeps me tossing and turning, though: Is this decision a sign of weakness or strength?

October 18 • FITTING IN IN THE OUTFIELD

I figured it couldn't hurt to talk to CJ. Even if it wasn't a good fit, she'd see I was trying to be a team player.

So at practice today, I asked CJ if I could talk to her in private.

"What's up, Soph?" she asked once we were alone.

"Well, with Lauren gone and all, I got to thinking. Maybe I can practice some outfield and see how it goes. I'd like to try, if you think that would be okay?" I asked hesitantly.

"Wow, Soph! That's a great idea. You can absolutely take some balls with the outfielders, and we'll see how it goes."

"Oh, okay. Cool. Thanks, Coach!" That wasn't how I'd expected it to go. I figured the conversation would mirror some of what I was feeling. Like disappointment, confusion, doubt, insecurity, or fear. But I didn't get any of that!

All the negative feelings festering inside me all week dissipated. After some BP, we moved into defensive groups, and instead of pitching with Teresa, I trotted to the outfield. Julie *immediately* threw me side-eye.

Being an outfielder takes rhythm. I warmed up with Yolanda and followed her lead working on crow hops. In the outfield, you can't simply set your feet and throw the ball. You have to get some momentum going and use your *whole* body to throw the ball longer distances—also known as a crow hop. It definitely took some coordination and time for me to adjust.

For footwork drills, CJ had us running back, shifting our feet from one side to the other, always looking over our shoulder, waiting for her to throw the ball. Again, it took some coordination, but I felt pretty good after a few tries.

We finally took the field, and CJ hit a mix of balls to the infield and outfield. She wanted us to work on throwing to different bases and hitting our cutoffs. Typically, if a ball is hit on the left side of the field, Zoe, our shortstop, is the cutoff, and if it is hit on the right side of the field, Becky, our second baseman, is the cutoff. More hit balls go to the shortstop than to any other position, so Zoe always needs to be ready.

Julie and I were in right field, Michelle Rafa in left, and Yolanda in center. Julie was not at *all* happy I was challenging her expected spot in the lineup. I know how badly she wants this opportunity . . . but so do I.

The first few practice rounds were routine fly balls and ground balls, throwing to second base. Then CJ challenged us by hitting ground balls. She wanted us to make one-hop throws to our catcher, Destiny, at home plate. Plays at home are pretty stressful, considering they can win or lose a game. Catchers not only have to snag the ball being fired at them, but they have a runner racing full steam at them, looking to bulldoze anyone who gets in the way of scoring. Throwing a perfect one-hop strike to the catcher is *really* important.

It took me a few rounds to figure out where to aim the bounce, but I threw with pretty good accuracy after that. I couldn't help but notice how much stronger I was throwing. I guess my workouts with Ellie were paying off . . . just not in the way I had anticipated.

Then CJ started working on balls over our heads and in the gap. Here is where rhythm and coordination really come into play. You have to run—no, sprint—backward while keeping focused on a moving ball flying from the opposite direction. Getting the right angle and running as smoothly as possible is key to catching that ball.

And given that my last attempt at this was at the Waves tryouts when I smacked into the wall, I surprised myself by how well I did. I was able to take good routes to balls to make sure they didn't get behind me, and I was able to track down balls I didn't think I could get to. I'm pretty fast, but don't get to use my speed much as a pitcher.

Flying all over the field during practice was amazing, and I didn't even feel winded. I was always ready for the next ball. Every time it was my turn, I mentally challenged CJ to hit to me. It's surprising how much mental preparation is involved in playing an outfield position. Dad always says softball is 90 percent mental, 10 percent physical. Playing a new position was definitely giving my brain a workout.

At one point, CJ pulled me aside. "You're really hustling out there and looking good. But here's a tip. As an infielder, it's a reaction to dive for anything close to you. Not the same story in the outfield, especially for a ball down the line." I remembered Dad telling me that before the Waves tryout, but never thought it would apply to me.

As we finished up our defensive practice, I started to feel like I'd been an outfielder all along. I'd never considered playing there before because I grew up feeling the outfield was where coaches hid the bad players. Most young players never hit the ball that far, so it's also super boring. But now that we're older, girls hit balls into the outfield all the time.

This could be the first day of something big. Maybe I'll be the one on *SportsCenter* one day!

October 20 · FRENEMIES

At school, I was in a good mood all morning. I'm pretty sure I even greeted my grumpy English teacher, Ms. Resnick, with a smile.

When I stopped at my locker before Language Arts, Casey slipped me a note:

> Meet me by our usual table at lunch today. I have something really important to talk to you about. ~ C

I nodded discreetly so she knew I read it. As I hurried to class, the worries started. *Did I do something wrong? Is Casey mad at me?* I tried to think back if I had forgotten to return a call or text. Casey can be overly dramatic sometimes, but I was pretty sure I hadn't done anything to tick her off.

I made sure not to dilly-dally and to get right to our table at the start of lunch. Casey's long ponytail came swinging around, and she bounced between people to get over to the table as quickly as she could.

Casey sat down and took a deep breath. "Thanks for getting here so fast. I've been dying to talk to you, and I know you had softball this weekend, so I thought I'd wait and talk to you in person."

"No problem. What's up?" I asked.

Other than being out of breath, I really couldn't tell if Casey was mad, sad, or excited. All I could tell was that this was going to be a *serious* conversation, good or bad.

"Jason Brooks" was all she said with a straight face.

Caught off guard and slightly confused, I said, "Jason Brooks? What about him?"

"What about him? How do you not know what I'm talking about?" She paused for a second to give me a chance to let it sink in. Once she realized that wasn't going to happen, she rolled her eyes and started from the beginning. "I mean, you know how much I like him, and the fall dance is coming up, and I thought for sure that he would've asked me by now, and he hasn't, and now I'm totally freaking out! What if he likes someone else? What if he's already asked someone else? This is great! Just great! My life is over!"

I was still stuck at "I like him." Casey talks so dang fast when she gets excited that it can be challenging to keep up sometimes. I guess I should have picked up on how much she liked Jason after meeting him at the mall. She did talk about him a lot, but I didn't think about it too much. *Clearly* not as much as she did.

"Casey, calm down. Your life is not over. You don't even know if he likes you or doesn't like you or if he likes someone else, or whatever you just said, so just take a deep breath." I think that may have helped, since her shoulders relaxed. "So when is the dance, anyway?"

Casey rolled her eyes at me again. "Hello! I've only been talking about this nonstop for the past two weeks! It's next weekend!"

"Oh, right. I probably forgot because I have a big game next weekend. Against the Waves." She didn't react. "THE WAVES." I waved my arms. "Only the team that cut me before I even had a chance to prove myself."

Casey didn't seem to get the import of this pronouncement.

"You won't believe what happened at practice yesterday," I continued. "I played the outfield! I know you're looking at me like, *You're not an outfielder. You're a pitcher!*" As I talked, I watched the movie of my successful career as an outfielder play out in my mind. Then my eyes met Casey's.

"What?" I asked, trying to navigate her glare.

"What does that have to do with Jason Brooks? Why does EVERYTHING always have to be about softball? This is a big deal to me, and all you can think about is softball! Do you know how many times I've sat and listened to you talk about softball? Most of the time I don't even know what you're talking about, but I'm your best friend, so I listen. Why can't you, *for once*, be a friend and listen to me and *my* stuff?"

I sat there with my mouth open, stunned.

"Just forget it!" she yelled as she stormed off.

When I got home, I relayed the conversation to Ellie as we fixed a snack in the kitchen. "I don't get it. I was stressing all day because I thought I'd done something wrong, only to learn that I didn't do anything wrong, but by the end of the conversation, I really *did* do something wrong." I stirred the mac 'n' cheese a little too vigorously.

"Sophia, not everyone's life revolves around softball. You and Casey have been friends forever, and she's a big part of your life too, and because of that, whatever is important to her should be important to you too. She seemed to want some advice, and all she got was an earful about crow hops."

I hate how logical and honest Ellie is. But that's also what I love most about her, even if she doesn't always agree with me. Then I focused on the point: *What's important to Casey.* All Casey and I ever cared about was playing outside, movies, and imaginary games. Does this mean that now *boys* are important to her?

"I wasn't trying to ignore her, I just got sidetracked. Sometimes I feel like the dog from that Pixar movie *Up.* 'Squirrel!'" We both laughed at the similarities between me and the animated talking dog that's always distracted.

"No, seriously," I said as our laughter died down. "That practice has been on my mind all day, and when she mentioned the dance next weekend, my brain automatically went to the Waves game on Sunday."

Ellie shot me an understanding smile. "I get it, Soph. But sometimes you have to leave those thoughts in your head and focus on what she needs to discuss with you. It's called a filter." She nudged me in the ribs with her elbow. "Look, just message her, apologize, and make it right. She's a good friend, and you don't want to lose her over Jason Bourne."

"It's Jason Brooks, you dork." I giggled.

"Yeah. Whoever. Just figure out what you're going to say and don't ruin the mac 'n' cheese AGAIN!"

I looked down. The pasta was looking a little overcooked. "Okay, okay," I said.

After eating, finishing my homework, and plenty of time to think about what I would write, I finally settled on this:

Today, 6:44 PM

> Casey, I am so sorry about today. I know how important this is to you and how patient you have been to talk about it with me. You have been the best friend anyone could ask for, and you have always been there for me. I am hoping you will forgive me, and hopefully we can work through the situation tomorrow. Love you. Your BFF - Soph

About ten minutes later, this is what she responded with:

> Thanks, Soph. I may have overreacted a little today. You are a good friend too. It just seems like ever since you started playing on your new team, that's all you ever talk about. I just felt like you were forgetting about me. Let's talk tomorrow. ♥♥♥ - Casey

I feel a little better knowing that Casey has more or less forgiven me. What still bothers me, though, is that last part. That I'm forgetting about her. I have to admit, there is a part of what she said that's true. Not entirely, but a little bit. Going to a new school, becoming a middle-schooler, playing on a new softball team and in a new position; it's a lot of change all at once. Our "important things" are changing. She cares about boys and popularity, and I care about getting a good one-hopper to the catcher. Stuff is changing at home. I can't quite put my finger on it, but Casey is catching on to it, too.

October 28 • BIG WEEKEND: QUAKES VS. WAVES

Things are more or less back to normal with Casey. We met during breaks and lunch during the week, when we shared the latest gossip and our grievances over unforgiving teachers and the relentless homework they assign. I did my best to coach her through talking to Jason, but my lack of experience was evident. After she passed notes to him in math class and made subtle references to the dance, it became clear he wasn't going to the dance with *anyone*, and that he was excited Casey was going and looked forward to seeing her there. That made Casey feel better.

Ellie, Dad, and I worked out almost every day after school this week, preparing for my game against the Waves. While Ellie hit, I headed to the outfield to shag balls and practice my drills. I was able to run down some tough hits, and after the third catch or so, I started to blush because Dad and Ellie were cheering enthusiastically.

"Woot, woot!" yelled Ellie.

"Like a freight train," screamed Dad. Then, "Elbow up. Step into your throws," because he can't help but coach me. "Atta girl."

In the car on the ride home after practice, Ellie said, "I know I'm your sister, and I'm supposed to be nice to you, but also as a normal person, you were pretty awesome out there. I mean, you're as good as some of the girls on my team. I think you're really onto something, Soph. Like, for real."

I leaned over and rested my head on her shoulder with a smile on my face. There's no better feeling than making my family proud.

Late Saturday night I got a call from Casey swooning over the dance.

"I wish you would've gone! It was so fun. I hung out with Tiffany and her friends, and Jason asked me to slow dance! It was crazy!"

"That's awesome, Casey. I'm so happy you had a good time and that it worked out with Jason. What was it like hanging out with Tiffany?" I felt a pang of jealousy at the thought of her new friend.

"She's totally cool. She had this super cute pink sequin dress I would've *died* for. It was so sparkly with all the lights from the dance."

"Sounds cute," I said with my best attempt at enthusiasm. This new side of Casey was weirding me out. She never liked wearing dresses before, and now she'd *die* for a *pink sequin* dress??? "Well, I'm happy you had a good time. I have to get ready for bed, though. Big game tomorrow."

"Oh, right. Good luck. I'll see you Monday."

"Okay. Night."

I was happy that Casey went to the dance and had a good time, but at the same time, I couldn't imagine being there. It sounded awful. Slow dancing with a boy? I hoped we weren't drifting too far apart.

I went into the Waves game with the confidence I needed, thanks to Dad and Ellie. I was bummed they couldn't make it to the game, but they'd arranged to have extended family there to support me. Aunt Gloria, Mom's younger sister, brought three of my cousins and enough supplies to survive the entire weekend. I used to be embarrassed when my relatives rolled in with wagons carrying monster provisions, but now I know every outing is an excuse for a fiesta.

I burst with excitement when I saw today's lineup. I was hitting second and starting in right field! Yolanda is our next strongest outfielder behind Lauren, so it's natural CJ would move her from left field to center to replace Lauren. Since I'm the newbie to the outfield, CJ put me in right field and moved Michelle to left. Teams typically have their stronger outfielders in center and left, since most hitters are right-handed and will likely hit the ball into those fields. Right field doesn't get a whole lot of action . . . but at least it's more action than on the bench!

#	Player	Position
13	Zoe	SS
25	Sophia	RF
3	Charlotte	1st
99	Destiny	C
5	Kendall	3rd
11	Becky	2nd
10	Yolanda	CF
4	Michelle	LF
7	Teresa	P
-	SUBS	-
9	Lilly	IF
27	Julie	OF

Julie eyeballed the lineup and quickly turned away, obviously disappointed she was still on the bench. I wondered how she would handle this. Would she stay the friend I had in the dugout, or turn back into the snarky girl dissing her teammates?

"Gonna be great having you out there with us today," enthused Yolanda. "Just hope I can handle center half as well as Lauren."

Julie avoided me as she listened to other teammates support me. I felt a twinge of guilt, but also a little frustration. Even Lilly, who also shared the bench with us, was being supportive. Isn't that what a team is for?

Teresa grabbed my shoulders and said, "You're gonna do great today. You've been awesome at practice, and we're going to show the Waves what they missed."

"Thanks, Teresa," I responded, trying my best to play it cool. We both wanted to prove Coach Adam made a mistake in cutting us from the team.

Both the Quakes and the Waves made strong defensive plays in the early innings. I hit the ball well my first at bat, but unfortunately, it went straight to Kristy in center field. My heart sank when she easily grabbed it for the out and fired the ball back to the infield.

In the top of the third inning, Zoe worked her short-game magic, slapping a high chopper over the third baseman's head for a base hit. Carefully monitoring Amanda on the pitcher's mound, Zoe inched toward second base. Amanda turned back repeatedly to keep an eye on her, but as soon as she released the next pitch, Zoe made a quick jump. In a matter of seconds, she slid in and stole second base.

Our team exploded in a cheer:

> *Extra, extra!*
> *Read all about it:*
> *Zoe stole second,*
> *And we wanna shout it!*

The energy was off the charts.

And then I was up again. I thought about Dad's advice: *Fake it until you make it.* I really wanted to show that I not only deserved to be there, but that we were better than the Waves. As the newest team in the league, we were definitely the underdogs, but I still wanted to win!

As I stepped into the batter's box, a monologue played in my head. *You are the best hitter ever. This pitcher has nothing on you. Hey, pitcher, I dare you to pitch it anywhere close to the strike zone. I dare you, and you'll see me knock it out of this park!*

I stared Amanda down, silently challenging her. I couldn't wait for the pitch, because I knew I was going to hit it hard and score Zoe. Amanda wound up, and the pitch looked like a big yellow grapefruit coming at me chest high. I symbolically licked my chops and loaded my swing. I was going to put this ball over the fence.

But then the ball began to rise, and it was too late to stop. I had already begun my swing, and when my bat connected with the ball, it was too far under it. I popped out to Tasha, the Waves' shortstop, to end the inning.

Shoot! I really wanted that hit. I was so frustrated. I'd had the opportunity to prove to everyone I was good enough. I'd had the chance to put the first run against the Waves on the board. I'd had the chance to show Kristy she underestimated me. And I failed.

I bet CJ was wondering whether she should pull me out of the game. I bet she thought what a mistake she'd made putting me in the lineup. And I bet Coach Adam thought he was right to cut me from the Waves roster.

I shook off the negative thoughts. It was time for me to get to the outfield and play defense. I couldn't afford to make any mistakes just because I was throwing a pity party for myself. Teresa confidently stepped up to the pitcher's mound.

The Waves' leadoff hitter was Olivia, and she took some notes from Zoe by laying down a good bunt to get on base. The next girl, Rosie, sacrifice-bunted Olivia over to second, and then it was Kristy Major's turn at bat. She stepped up to the plate with a smug look on her face. There was no way I would allow her a base hit.

Unlike me, Kristy was patient in the batter's box. She was looking for her pitch, not just any pitch. She took a ball, and then a strike. She hits lefty even though she throws right, like me, but I could tell she wanted to knock it out, not slap or bunt it, because she wasn't moving in the box at all.

Teresa's next pitch was low and inside, and Kristy sent the ball sailing down the right field line. I got a really good jump on it and was quickly gaining speed. My natural competitiveness kicked in as I desperately tried to stop Kristy from getting on base. Instinctively, I dove for the ball.

The moment I hit the ground with an empty glove, I felt the pain of my error.

Knowing there was no one to back me up, I scrambled back to my feet pronto to chase the ball down, but was only quick enough to hold Kristy to a triple. She mockingly gave me a thumbs-up.

Kristy's hit brought Olivia home, and just like that, the Waves scored a run and were in the lead—because of me. The good feels of the day quickly evaporated.

Tears welled in my eyes, and it took everything I had to hold back a full-blown cry, especially with my aunt and cousins sitting on the line near me. No wonder the Waves didn't want me. I bet CJ was wondering why she picked me up too. I'll never be as good as Ellie, no matter where I am on the field.

The Waves scored three more runs, ending the inning 4–0. As we jogged in, CJ tried to make eye contact with me, but I avoided her because of the lump in my throat.

CJ immediately pulled me aside. *Oh, great. Here it is. She's going to bench me.*

"Sophia," she said. "Look at me."

As much as I was avoiding it, I looked up, but to my surprise, CJ had a slight smile on her face.

"It's okay, Sophia. I can tell you're beating yourself up for missing that ball. You made a rookie outfielder mistake. I mean, you haven't had much experience out there, but I'm the one who put you in. Do you know why?"

I couldn't bring myself to speak, afraid that a sob might slip out. So I just shook my head.

"Because what I saw at practice was raw, natural, awesome talent. You have an instinctual positive first step, which gives you a great jump on the ball as well as awesome speed to track down those balls. Diving for a ball down the line is a hard habit for a former infielder to break. Even though I talked to you about this at practice, it's tough to change that reaction. It will take time."

I was still unable to make eye contact, so she continued. " But that just shows me how much passion you have, Sophia. The best players are the ones that can bounce back after failure. We're all in this together. So get in the dugout and support your team. Okay?"

She patted me on the back before sprinting over to the third base coach's box. I was a little confused and surprised. I'd expected CJ to yell at me and bench me for making such a *huge* mistake. Not only didn't she do that, she told me how good I was. I remembered the speech Coach Adam gave at the Waves tryouts, the whole notion that you better play your best game at all times because you're replaceable. If I were a Wave and I'd made that mistake, he would've ousted me.

I replayed the conversation with CJ over and over in my head, through my at bats and play in the outfield. Something Coach said really resonated with me. *We're in this together.* Both my mistakes were partially because I was putting too much pressure on myself.

Like I had to win the game all on my own. I didn't need to make a grand play. I just needed to take a deeper angle to keep the ball in front of me.

It's impossible to win the game alone, and if I take away the pressure I put on myself, I'll be more relaxed and probably more successful too. On that note, I walked over to Julie as we watched our team bat. "Hey, Jules."

She glanced at me before she grabbed the fence, focusing on the players on the field. "Hey," she said, monotone.

"Are we okay? I mean, with me playing outfield now and all?"

"Yeah. Sure. It's fine. I mean, it's whatever." Still no eye contact.

"It's just that I really like you, and we've become friends, and I don't want this to come between us. That's really important to me."

She finally turned to face me as a smile slowly emerged. She touched my arm and said, "Don't worry, Soph. We're good. Yeah, of course I want to be out there, but you're right. We can't let lineups ruin a friendship."

"Okay, good. I'm so relieved. I wouldn't be able to do this if I knew you didn't have my back."

"Of course, Soph. I have your back."

I took a deep breath. That had been weighing on me. We both turned our attention back to the game and cheered on our teammates. I felt a shift in her attitude too.

Julie and I went crazy when YoYo got on with a base hit up the middle and Lilly came in to pinch-run for her. I'm sure it was to give Lilly some game time, but we weren't able to put enough hits together to score her. Tough break.

Teresa came out and fought hard, with our defense fighting just as hard behind her. Zoe made a few awesome diving plays, and I tracked down a deep fly ball with a runner in scoring position to end the inning. As a team, we shut the Waves down from scoring any more runs.

Despite the good feels in the dugout, and some impressive playing from my teammates, we ended up losing to the Waves 4–0. It's not that we played *badly*. We fought hard. We just couldn't get our base runners in. Every time a runner would get on or in scoring position, we choked. We couldn't put all the pieces of the puzzle together.

What I learned, however, is that instead of being afraid to fail, as CJ put it, failure can help you learn and grow. I'm *supremely* bummed we lost, but hopeful about working on my game and our team working together.

October 31 • HALLOWEEN & DÍA DE LOS MUERTOS

Mom, Ellie, and I had to run errands after school. We'd been procrastinating about buying Halloween candy and all of our Día de los Muertos decorations, so we decided to get it all done at once.

"Okay, we need at least two big bags of candy,"

Mom said, referring to her list, "colored tissue paper for the paper flowers, tablecloths with sugar skulls, sugar skull plates and napkins, pan dulce, and more candles. I think that should be it. I have all of the food ingredients, and Aunt Eileen will be bringing stuff too."

"Make sure you get the good Halloween candy. No one wants the cheapo stuff," Ellie said as she perused the candy aisle for options.

"What are we having for Día de los Muertos, other than pan dulce?" I asked, referring to the sweet pastries I loved.

"Aunt Eileen is bringing empanadas, and I'm making sopa de azteca, frijoles, and of course Mexican hot chocolate."

I started to salivate just thinking about the treats. Besides Christmas, Día de los Muertos, which coincides with Halloween, is my favorite holiday. Nearby, an enthusiastic woman was providing details about the Day of the Dead to her young sons. I remembered being captivated by all the colorful skulls and skeletons when I was their age.

"It's a Mexican celebration," the woman began, "where the souls of those who are dead come back and join their loved ones on Earth for a big party." The boys' eyes were wide. "Later, we'll set up an altar with offerings like candles, flowers, and food. We'll put out pictures of Nana Lil and Papi John, and others who passed, to help them find their way home." The boys looked at each other with anticipation.

"So what are your plans tonight, Sis? The usual?" Ellie asked, holding a skull mask in front of her face.

"Yeah." I laughed, pretending to be spooked. Halloween wasn't as predictable this year as I had thought, though.

It's been a tradition that Casey and I have a sleepover on Halloween, even if it's a school night. After trick-or-treating, we watch classic films like *Halloween* and *The Shining* to scare ourselves silly, and we sleep with all the lights in the house blazing. We'd scream so loud that her parents poked their heads in repeatedly to remind us to be quiet. Regardless of how frightened we were, we looked forward to this night every year, which is why I was surprised when Casey suggested we go to the Haunted House Night at one of the high schools instead.

"Come on, Soph! *Everyone's* going to be there! Well, that's what Tiffany told me. I bet a bunch of crazy stuff is going to happen, and we'll be the only ones in the entire school that will miss it. Just think of all the inside jokes everyone is going to be talking about, and we'll be standing there looking like the idiots who miss out on everything!"

Leave it to Casey to be overly dramatic. "I'm sure we'll survive, Casey. Tiffany will still like you even if you don't go. Besides, I love our Halloween sleepover. Won't you miss it too?" We could do both, but it takes so much effort to be around new people. When it's just Casey and me, it's easy.

"Well, yeah. But we're in middle school now. Aren't we too old for trick-or-treating?"

"Who says? What if I don't like or care what everyone else does? I think our tradition is perfectly fine, no matter what grade we're in.

Besides, there've been enough changes in my life lately, and I could really use some normal time with my bestie." I pouted, going for full sympathy vote.

"Ugggg! Fine! Guilt me into it. But the next big thing that comes up, you're coming with me, like it or not. Deal?"

"Deal!"

What a relief. There's something about sixth grade that reminds me of those schools of fish that are always in perfect formation, all moving together in the same direction at the same exact time. I feel like I'm the fish that missed the memo, and I'm swimming in the exact opposite direction. Either that, or I'm the one that slams into everyone else, ruining the whole formation.

I mean, who writes these rules, anyway? Who says that we have to dress this way, and be this size, and talk like this? Someone at some point proclaimed this is what we must do, and we not only follow along, but we all enforce the rules. We're the first ones to point out when someone steps out of line. Can't everyone else see they're all just blending in? They are part of one big school of fish without a single one standing out from the rest.

Casey dressed as a zombie, mostly because she didn't want anyone to recognize her trick-or-treating, especially Jason. I dressed as Lisa Fernandez, my favorite softball player, who won three gold medals for Team USA. When Ellie was eleven, she went to a Lisa Fernandez clinic, and she and Mom made a jersey with "Fernandez" on the back with the number 16 and USA written on the front. She even got it signed. Lisa is Hispanic too, so putting my dark hair up with a visor made me look the part.

"Trick-or-treat!" we squealed as we rang each doorbell on the street. Neighbors opened their front doors and acted both terrified and delighted as they dropped assorted treats in our bags. After collecting about a pound of candy each, we came home, ate pizza, and swapped goodies. I'm partial to Milky Ways, and Casey traded

hers for my mini-boxes of gummy bears and SweeTarts. Our love of sweets hasn't diminished since the first day we met. We settled into a marathon of horror movies, which culminated with *Nightmare on Elm Street*.

After hours of horror films, the nightmarish scenes got the best of us, and we took a stress-relieving break. I was starting to relax when Casey glanced at the window and froze.

"Did you see that?" she screeched.

"What?" I looked hesitantly at the darkened window.

"That! A guy with a Taser hook!" She grabbed her chest and fell over.

Truly concerned, I ran to her side to see what was the matter.

"Gotcha!" She laughed as she sprang to her feet. Clearly, she delighted in nearly scaring the life out of me.

Once my heart started beating normally again, Casey changed the subject to Jason, who she was happy to talk about, and I pretended to be happy to talk about him as well. I even teased her a little when I chased her around the house with bright, red-stained lips from my cherry sucker, saying, "Oh, darling Casey! I am so in love with you! Muah, muah, muah!"

Casey's communication with Jason exists mostly through text. I don't think they have many face-to-face conversations. As long as you're "talking" to a boy, you're cool, but an actual relationship isn't necessary. It's hard to keep track of the rules sometimes.

Even though I don't really care to talk about Jason, it was fun hanging out with Casey, like old times. I know we're growing up, but there's a part of me that never wants to grow out of simple nights like this. Maybe I should track down the person who writes the rules (maybe it's Tiffany) and see if they can just let this one slide.

November 4 · QUAKES VS. PUMAS & BATBUSTERS

I was so excited both Mom and Dad had the weekend off. Not only did they get to see me play, but we drove to Yorba Linda together. It was like old times—all of us in Dad's truck talking pregame strategy.

"Don't stand like a statue out there. Stay on the balls of your feet so you're always ready to run," Dad coached me as we exited the freeway.

We got to the fields at the same time as CJ and Teresa, who spilled out of their Bimmer and ran over to me.

"Sophia, we stopped at Starbucks and bought your favorite! Caramel macchiato Frappuccino," Teresa said with a smile.

"Oh, my god! Thanks so much. This looks delicious, and I could use it to wake me up after that long drive!"

Teresa put her arm through mine, and we headed toward the fields.

"Sophia! Are you forgetting something?" Dad yelled from the car, holding up my bat bag.

"Oh, yeah. Right." I hustled back to the car and grabbed my bag. He asked about my drink.

"It's a caramel macchiato Frappuccino," I answered.

"A caramel mocky whata?"

"Dad! Don't hurt yourself." I giggled at his attempt to repeat the name. "It's a cold coffee drink."

"You're drinking coffee now? !Ay, Chihuahua!" I rolled my eyes and started to walk away. "You know, they say that'll stunt your growth!" he shouted after me, laughing.

Teresa and I sipped our Frappuccinos in the dugout and caught up on our week, waiting for the rest of the team. Conversation flows so easily with her. She's like Ellie and Casey combined. She has lots of friends at school and after-school activities, but she also has this whole softball superstar alter ego. I don't know how she balances it all, but I can learn a thing or two from her.

Once the rest of the team arrived, we jogged around the bases, stretched, and warmed up. Teresa and I were throwing together when she said, "You know, I've been meaning to tell you how awesome you are."

"What do you mean?" I asked with some confusion.

"Moving into the outfield and everything. You saw we needed help, and you stepped in. Plus, you're killing it out there. It's hard to switch positions like that. I'm so happy you're on our team."

I'm sure I blushed a little bit. "Aw! Teresa, I'm happy too. I've always loved softball." I looked around at everyone throwing. "But I'm so pumped now. I feel like this season has really taken it to a whole new level. Didn't think that was even possible."

When we got back into the dugout, CJ posted the lineup. I was hitting second and playing right field. I glanced down the line at my parents, excited this would be their first time seeing me play with the Quakes. Mom got her scorebook ready. She always keeps score, even if she isn't the official scorekeeper.

Dad wasn't next to Mom, though. There was only one other spot he might be. I looked behind home plate. As expected, he was setting up his camera.

Even though he's not our official coach anymore, he still likes to review game footage with me and Ellie. At times, his "input" can be a little overbearing, but he definitely knows his stuff. He totally could have been a pro player, and I think he regrets not playing in college. That's why he pushes Ellie and me so hard in school and softball. He wants us to have opportunities he didn't have.

We played our first game against the Pacoima Pumas, and I was happy with my outfield play. I caught a tough foul ball off the fence and threw a girl out at home on a base-hit ground ball. *You thought you could score on me from second base! Ha! I don't think so!*

I could have done a little better hitting. I got on base two out of three times, but didn't feel like I connected well with the ball. The whole team hit like that. When we got runners in scoring position, we froze and either struck out or popped up.

The Quakes and Pumas were tied 0–0 going into the sixth inning. Then the Pumas' leadoff hitter got a base hit up the middle and was bunted over to second. Next, their sturdy third baseman hit a fly ball to center. It looked like it was a routine fly heading straight to Yolanda. But she completely misread the ball and ran in. When I saw that, I freaked out and yelled, "Back! Back!" but it was too late. The ball flew way over her head. That hit scored the first Puma hitter for the only run in the game. And we lost . . . again.

The loss wasn't the way we wanted to start today's doubleheader. CJ must have thought the same thing. With another game to go, she called us together for a pep talk.

"You guys aren't believing in yourselves out there," CJ began. "You're hitting like individuals, and when the pressure's on, you're putting too much pressure on yourselves to be the hero. Let me ask you this: How many of you, when you step up to the plate with a runner on, picture yourself hitting a huge bomb to the outfield? Hitting a double or a triple or maybe even a home run?"

We looked around, and slowly, everyone raised their hands.

"See! That's what I mean. You don't have to be the hero, to win it all with one swing. I want you to think *one* base at a time. That's it. If we *all* hit for one base at a time, we'll have more overall runs. Now raise your hand if you believe in your team?" We all raised our hands. "Look around. Look at that support and encouragement. I want you to take that with you when you step into the batter's box. You all wear a uniform because you're alike. Inside that uniform, you're part of a group—no one is above or below anyone else in the same uniform."

I looked down at my green-and-gold jersey and around at these girls. My uniform is like a coat of armor—it identifies and protects me; it makes me and my teammates greater than any individual. And my teammates are like a shield—we defend and help one another. We all want the same thing. And we'll have a much better chance of winning if we work together. It'll be a lot more fun too.

CJ posted the lineup for the next game against the Batbusters, and I couldn't believe it when I saw she moved me from right to center field. I wondered how YoYo would react moving back to left field, but just then, someone grabbed me from behind and gave me a noogie.

"All right, Sophia. Large and in charge out there today!" Yolanda joked.

"Thanks. I may need you to give me some pointers."

"No way. You got this, chica!" She gave me a high five. I was relieved she was so supportive. I immediately ran to tell Dad the news.

"Way to go, kiddo," he said proudly. "That's a lot more responsibility out there in center. Your teammates are going to look to you to take command of the field. They're going to listen for you to remind them of the outs, where they're going with the ball, and overall support when your team needs it. You're the leader of the outfield now." He patted my shoulder, as if saying, *That's my girl!*

"I know, Dad. I won't let them down."

"I know you won't. Go get 'em!"

#	Player	Position
13	Zoe	SS
25	Sophia	CF
3	Charlotte	1st
99	Destiny	C
5	Kendall	3rd
11	Becky	2nd
10	Yolanda	LF
4	Michelle	RF
7	Teresa	P
-	SUBS	-
9	Lilly	IF
27	Julie	OF

CJ's pep talk helped us find our mojo again, because we took a one-run lead against the Batbusters in the third inning. And at the end of each inning, I couldn't wait to get back in the outfield. Sometimes I felt like a cheetah out there. I even made a diving catch! It was awesome to have a successful play after my disastrous dive down the line against the Waves.

Even though it was weeks ago, and CJ let me off the hook, I'm still super pissed about missing that ball, especially since it was Kristy at bat. If the roles were reversed, Kristy never would've missed it.

Given the unseasonable heat of the day, we all struggled a bit as the afternoon wore on. Five- or six-hour-long doubleheaders can be tough on players—sometimes even tougher on fans sitting in the stands. Between the fourth and fifth innings of the second game, I looked around the field and for a moment, it felt like time stood still.

But then I was snapped back to reality.

"Are you out of your mind?" the Batbusters' coach yelled at his pitcher. The coach, a short guy with an even shorter temper, was a yeller, which usually gets the opposite results from those intended. "If you don't strike the next hitter out, you're on the bench!" His yelling forced the pitcher to constantly second-guess her choices. She wasn't the only Batbuster embarrassed by being singled out for her mistakes.

The BBs really seemed to struggle, and I could tell the players didn't want to be the next yelled at, so they started blaming the umpire. In the fourth inning after we'd scored two more runs, the BBs' third baseman was up to bat and struck out. To our surprise, she started arguing with the umpire, which is a HUGE no-no.

"Are you freaking kidding me? That wasn't even close to a strike!" she yelled at home plate for everyone to see and hear.

Her coach marched down from the third-base coaching box. All of us assumed it was to control his player, but OH, NO! He started laying into the umpire as well, and even some of the Batbuster parents sitting behind the dugout chimed in. I thought the coach was going to get ejected from the game, but the first base umpire defused the situation by sending the coach and his player back to their dugout.

After we got the other two outs, we ran off the field as usual, but CJ had a few words to share before we went in to hit.

"What you all saw out there on the field from both the Busters' player and coach was unacceptable. I hope I never see any of you behave that way, and I hope you never see me behave that way, either. These umpires are doing their best, and they're tired and hot just like we are. Yes, some are better than others, but they're human. As players and coaches, it's important for us to only worry about what we can control. Kendall, can you control whether or not you swing at a pitch?"

"Um, yes." Caught off guard, Kendall responded as though it was a trick question.

"Do you have control over whether or not the umpire calls a ball or a strike?"

Again, CJ directed her question to Kendall, who wiped the sweat from her brow. "Um, no."

"Right! And that's exactly why you should never waste your energy getting upset about it. Not to mention that's horrible sportsmanship. We'll come across teams, players, coaches, and even family members who are disrespectful and rude, and I just want to make it clear that behavior like that will not be tolerated. Are we clear on this?"

"YES," we all said together.

"Okay, then. Let's get in that dugout and show them how a team with class wins a game! 'Hit, run, score' on three! One, two, three . . ."

"HIT, RUN, SCORE!"

And we did just that. The umpire made a few questionable calls, but we took the calls, moved on, and came out with the win.

Final score: Quakes 5—Batbusters 3.

⚾

Hot, sweaty, and tired, I felt good sitting in Dad's truck with the windows wide open on the ride home. But just as I began to relax, Dad started with his input.

"You know, I think there's something going on with your hands at the start of your swing," he announced like he was onto something important.

"Seriously, Dad? I just finished playing two long games in the hot sun, made a diving catch, I might add, and I went five for nine at bat, which isn't too bad. And one of the times I got out was because you called a changeup and it wasn't a changeup and it totally threw me off."

Dad is pretty good at calling pitches, whether he picks them off the coaches or is able to catch it from the pitcher's grip. Since he's usually watching from behind the plate, we have a secret code that he'll call out when he thinks a changeup is coming. Every once in a while, he misses the pitch, though, which totally messes me up. "Why do you always have to point out what I did wrong?" I said.

"Hey, hey, hey!" Mom intervened, glaring at Dad out of the corner of her eye. "Sophia, you know your dad. He's trying to help you be the best you can be. That being said, I think we should make a new rule. No criticism—constructive or otherwise—on the ride home. Let Sophia decompress after a hard day of playing, and we can talk fundamentals later."

Mom looked optimistically back and forth between Dad and me. She's always the peacemaker. She never graduated high school and only has her GED, but I think if she'd been able to go to college, she could have been a great diplomat.

I shot back, "Well, if we're making new rules, what about the videos? Dad, I think you should let me come to you when I'm ready to watch them, rather than you show them to me the second we get home from the game."

With a sigh, he said, "Okay, mija. I just think looking at the footage is the best way to learn. But if that's what you want." His shoulders drooped a little as he gripped the steering wheel.

"Well, good news, bad news," Mom broke in. "You don't have to worry about Dad overstepping next month."

"What do you mean?" I asked.

"Papi and I are taking on some weekend shifts, so we're going to miss more games. I already mentioned it to CJ, and she said you're welcome to stay with them the next few weekends."

As much as I love hanging out with Teresa, I was speechless. They needed to pick up shifts, which is code for "we're in financial trouble," which always stresses me out.

Plus, I felt like a brat now, telling Dad I didn't want his help. I really do want his help. His timing is just off sometimes, and I mostly spoke out of frustration. Now he won't even be at my games to give me feedback.

We spent the rest of the car ride in silence. I really wanted to say, *Okay, Dad, give me feedback. Let's watch the videos when we get home. I'm sorry.* But my overwhelming stubbornness didn't allow me to say those words out loud.

QUAKES FASTPITCH

**Please join us for a car wash supporting
the Quakes softball team**
SATURDAY
10:00 A.M. – 4:00 P.M.
McDonald's Parking Lot, Moorpark Plaza
Thanks for your support!

November 5 • CAR WASH

Today we organized a car wash as a team fundraiser. We made posters to display on the street corners and custom T-shirts for everyone on the team.

Washing cars for hours sounds grueling, but it was another unseasonably warm day, and we had a blast getting into water fights. As we were hanging up posters, Teresa, Julie, and I created a cheer.

D - I - R - T - Y

Dirty car, no need to cry.

Get your car washed nice and clean.

Come on down; support our team!

We even choreographed some moves and stood in a kick line with Teresa and me on the ends and Julie in the middle. With each beat, Teresa and I stood tall while Julie squatted down, and then we switched. However, since we have the worst rhythm ever, we kept messing up. Julie performed a curtsy to acknowledge the imaginary applause.

"We are the best cheerleaders ever," Julie said, wiping tears from her face from laughing. "People should get a car wash because they feel sorry for us."

I finally had to smush my cheeks in because they hurt so much from smiling. Julie and Teresa looked at me like I was crazy, and I had to incoherently plead with them to stop because my cheeks hurt so badly.

Zoe skipped over with her crimped side ponytail as if we were at an 80s-themed car wash. "I didn't realize holding signs on a street corner could be so fun, or I would've taken this job instead of washing cars."

We tried to explain why we were laughing so hard, but she just rolled her eyes.

"I guess it's one of those *you had to be there* type of deals," Zoe said, amused. "Speaking of which, I'm hoping you guys can take a break from your *excellent* cheerleading to help me out with a prank on CJ." Zoe is a total prankster—she's been warming up with little pranks all season. But this was going to be bigger.

The plan was for Yolanda, Kendall, and Destiny to distract CJ talking softball strategy while we sabotaged her. As YoYo and Destiny jabbered on about first and third plays, the four of us crept up behind CJ and doused her with cold, soapy water. Coach arched her back and let out a high-pitched scream. The four of us ran while the other girls aimed their hoses on her. Just as CJ wiped the soapy water from her face, she opened her mouth, probably to reprimand us, and the water from the hoses nailed her right in the face.

Defeated, CJ spit a mouthful of water out like a fish fountain.

"Okay. Who put you guys up to this?" CJ asked, scanning all of us. We glanced in Zoe's direction as we tried to contain our laughter, but once CJ figured it out, she shouted, "I knew it! I'm going to get you for this!"

Zoe took off running. It was clear CJ didn't have a shot at catching her, and CJ quickly gave up. "Okay, fine. You just wait!"

After it seemed we washed all the dirty cars in Moorpark, CJ rewarded us all with ice cream. I got three scoops and ate one flavor at a time, from lightest to darkest, starting with vanilla, moving on to coffee, and ending with chocolate.

We were so delighted by the break that no one suspected what came next. CJ nonchalantly walked by, and just as Zoe was about to take a bite of her cone, CJ playfully tapped it, so a blob of vanilla stuck to Zoe's nose. Trying to lick the frozen treat off her face, Zoe theatrically chased CJ around the shop in retaliation. Which, of course, made her scoop fall on Lilly and Michelle, which was when all havoc broke loose and we got into a huge ice cream fight. As the ice cream melted, we slurped it off our hands and fingers, but it still left a sticky mess. Thank goodness we had hoses to clean ourselves up afterward.

The day symbolized what a team sport is for me. Here we were, being silly, getting in food fights, pranking one another, and having so much fun our laughter echoed all around us. It doesn't matter what neighborhood we live in, what our ethnicity is, what type of clothes we wear. As long as we play softball, nothing else matters. It feels great to have the freedom to be ourselves. It's how I've always felt around Casey . . . until recently. I hope that never changes. That we can be who we are when we're together—not who other people want us to be.

When the afternoon was over, we counted all the proceeds and banked two hundred and fifty dollars! This is money we can use toward tournament fees, gas, meals, and other stuff that costs a lot, and it helps families like mine that don't have a lot of extra money to spend.

I was super tired after the car wash and felt like chilling, but I was staying the night at Teresa's, and she wanted to go to a movie. The Westlake multiplex is near the mall, and CJ offered to treat us to a mani/pedi beforehand.

I rarely paint my nails—which are mostly chewed to the nub—and I've never paid someone to paint them for me. And I also have only watched a real movie in a theater a few times. I love films, but mostly we just watch them at home. Since we don't have cable, Ellie and I have a stack of old DVDs we watch over and over. So this was going to be a special night.

"So, Sophia, what kind of manicure do you want?" CJ asked as we entered the nail salon. "Gel? Acrylic? I wouldn't recommend acrylic while you're playing, but gels hold up pretty well."

"Are those colors?" I asked.

"No, silly," Teresa scoffed. "They're types of manicures. You know, like acrylic are those fake nails that are really long, and gels are a super hard polish that lasts way longer than regular polish."

"Oh, um. I'll just do whatever you're doing," I said. "If it's good for playing in, I'll try it." It was hard not to seem out of place.

"Wow, your first mani-pedi! I want you to really enjoy this," said CJ. "Why don't you get started, and I'll run next door and get some drinks. The usual? Caramel macchiato Frappuccino?"

"Yeah, Mom! That sounds great!" Teresa replied. She turned to me. "So do you want a color or French?"

¡Ay, Chihuahua! More cryptic choices! "Um, whatever you're

doing." I was beginning to sweat with all these choices.

After selecting Stormy Blue polish for my fingernails and toes, and tiny adhesive stars for accents, we settled into giant leather chairs to soak our feet in a mini Jacuzzi bath. The chairs actually vibrated to feel like a massage! Sipping my Frappuccino, soaking my tired feet, having a massage, I thought, *I could get used to this!*

"Oh, Teresa, I forgot to mention that Caleb called earlier," CJ casually mentioned with a wink.

"Mom, it's not what you think. He's also going to a movie tonight, so probably just trying to coordinate." My heart skipped a beat when she said "coordinate." As in, we'd be meeting up—with boys?

"Okay, good, because last I heard, you were kind of talking to Josh," CJ said slyly. "It's hard to keep up with your love life."

"Well, then, stop trying so hard," Teresa said, looking part annoyed and part amused.

"So what's happening?" I interjected, trying to muffle my sense of panic.

"Some friends are seeing a movie tonight, and I thought we could all meet up. I hope you don't mind. They're really cool."

"I'm sure they are. That's the problem. I am *so not* really cool. I mean, I just don't relate to boys really well."

"Oh, it'll be fine," CJ reassured me. "They're sweet boys. Teresa has been friends with them since preschool. Just be yourself. You'll all get along great."

"Right. Just be myself. The super awkward girl who knows nothing about how to communicate with teenage boys, but sure, I'm sure it'll be fine," I said, half to them and half to myself. I leaned back into my massage chair and tried to get the whole chill vibe back. But I was so tense, the vibrating rollers bounced my body around like a pinball machine.

I looked over at CJ and Teresa, whose eyes were closed as they settled into a state of pure bliss. I tried to mimic them and breathe deeply, but it took a little time to feel like I wasn't being beaten up by the chair.

We got to the theater early to make sure we could find Caleb and his friends. I was so self-conscious, and annoyed at myself for being bothered so much. I've never cared much about how I look, and now all of a sudden, I was second-guessing everything about my appearance. Were my eyebrows too thick? Did my jeans make me look fat? Is my vintage *Sandlot* T-shirt cool or too tomboyish? ¡Ay!

"There they are!" Teresa whispered in my ear when the boys arrived. I couldn't help noticing the small pendant hanging from her neck on a golden chain. It looked like some sort of a softball charm—a tiny home plate with an inscription.

"Sophia, these are my friends Michael, Alex, and Caleb," Teresa said when they approached.

"Hi," I muttered almost inaudibly. I wasn't sure if I was supposed to shake their hand or give them a hug, knucks, or curtsy. I couldn't think that quickly, so it ended up being an awkward wave, like a dead fish flapping on the end of my arm.

They gave me a nod and mumbled some variation of "hey," "hi," "hello." Well, at least they didn't laugh. I desperately wanted to chew on a nail but didn't want to ruin my fresh manicure.

Okay, I survived the introduction, so hopefully, we'd sit down inside the theatre and be done talking. But there were at least thirty minutes of ads and previews before the film, which made time for more awkward small talk. I sat between Teresa and Caleb. Teresa was busy chatting with Michael—which left me either to talk to Caleb or stare at the ceiling.

My initial instinct was to try to channel Teresa's or Casey's flirtatious nature, but that isn't me.

"You like *The Sandlot*, huh?" Caleb asked, referring to my T-shirt.

"Yeah, it's one of my all-time favorite movies. That, *The Wizard of Oz*, and *A League of Their Own*."

"Yeah, I like *A League of Their Own* too. So do you play softball with Teresa?"

"Yeah. I'm on her team, the Quakes. Do you play?"

"Yeah, baseball. I play center. You?"

"Me too! Well, I just started playing outfield. I didn't think I'd like it, but I really do."

"Yeah, it's pretty awesome. I love tracking down balls and robbing home runs." He puffed out his chest.

"Well, I don't know if I'm quite to Mike Trout status yet, but I'm working on it."

"You know who Mike Trout is?" he asked, shocked.

"Of course I do."

"Huh. I don't think I've ever met a girl who knows who he is. He's my favorite MLB player."

"No kidding? Well, he's great, but too bad he's not a Dodger," I teased.

"What! No way. Angels all the way."

I giggled as I replied, "Well, either way, he can rob some serious home runs. Do you know who Caitlin Lowe is? She played

for Arizona in college, Team USA, and the Florida Pride in the professional league. She's robbed some crazy hits too in her time."

"Yeah, she's crazy fast. I can't believe how quick she can get down the line. I actually watched one of her games on TV when she played for the Pride."

"Yeah—National Pro Fastpitch. I'd love to play in that league one day."

"That's when I got hooked on softball. It was really fun to watch her. Definitely one of the greatest outfielders."

He talked with such enthusiasm, I thought he might knock his soda over. Most guys don't know or care about softball, so I was super impressed. I was about to go on about more of my favorite players when the lights dimmed for the movie. My disappointment shocked me. When we first sat down, I thought it was going to be an agonizing wait, and now I was wishing we had more time to talk. I guess CJ was right. Just being me isn't too bad after all.

(My ticket from the movie)

NOVEMBER 6 • TROUBLE ON DECK

Last night turned out to be a lot of fun. All the pressure of "following the rules" was what was making me so nervous. It's a whole lot easier to just toss out the rules and do me.

Teresa and I woke up early for softball, and her mom stopped by Starbucks on the way to the fields to pick up iced blended coffees.

"How did it go?" CJ asked.

"Yeah, Sophia! How did it go?" Teresa said with a nudge.

"What? It went fine."

"Yeah, I think Caleb thought it went fine too," Teresa teased.

"So you and Caleb hit it off, huh?" CJ asked knowingly.

"No! We just got along. He likes baseball and softball—and *The Sandlot*, apparently. So we just talked about that kind of stuff." The blood rushed to my face. It wasn't because I liked him, but just the insinuation of a boy liking me freaked me out.

"Well, that's cool. You seemed a little nervous, so I'm glad you had a good time." Thankfully CJ changed the topic, and that was the end of THAT discussion. "I heard you have some guests coming to watch the game today, Sophia. Who all is going to be there?"

Coach glanced at me in the rearview mirror as she merged onto the freeway.

"Not sure. I think my aunt Eileen and uncle Joe might be coming from Long Beach. A few cousins too. Whoever's not busy. They live close by the park."

"You have *so* many relatives!" Teresa chimed in.

"Yeah." I laughed. "My cousins keep having babies—I can't even keep up with all the names. And when relatives visit from Mexico, there are cousins I haven't even met."

"That's great they come to support you. I'm sorry your parents couldn't make it this weekend, though," Coach said warmly.

"Yeah, they work a lot." I felt a hole in my stomach. Even though I was having fun, getting used to not having my parents at my games hasn't settled well with me. They've always been a big part of my softball experience, and playing without them just felt wrong.

Immediately I got angry at myself for resenting my parents for not coming to my games. I took a deep breath and a sip of my coffee. I mean, the whole reason they weren't at my games was because they're working to pay for Ellie and me to be able to play. So whenever those thoughts creep into my head, I try to focus on ways I can make them proud.

When we stepped out of the car, it was only eight in the morning, but it was already scorching hot. The weather forecast was for temperatures to be in the eighties by the afternoon, so we had to pace ourselves.

Our first game was against the Athletics, and I started in center field and hit second in the lineup. I don't think Yolanda minded moving back to left field. That's where she's used to playing, and she feels more comfortable there. Julie's been much more positive since our little chat. At least she *seems* more positive, and I hope that's truly how she feels even when I'm not in the dugout.

About fifteen minutes before the game started, my entourage arrived. A line of relatives carried beach umbrellas, chairs, canopies,

blankets, ice chests, and enough food for an army. It looked like they were moving in. Aunt Eileen slipped over to the dugout to greet me.

"Hi, sweetie. It's going to be a scorcher today, so I brought an ice chest with cold rags and squirt bottles to cool you guys down. Where should I put it?"

"Um, how about at the end of the dugout, up against the fence?"

"Of course, sweetheart! That's what your mom would've done." I felt the pang again. "We're so excited to watch you play.

I heard you're starting in center field now! That's an important position, right?"

"Yeah! I really like it. I'm front and center," I said with a giggle.

"Atta girl! Well, all right. Here you go." Aunt Eileen handed me a water bottle. "Make sure to drink lots of water and keep cool! ¡Buena suerte!" She motioned for my cousins to haul the cooler to the dugout while the extended Garcia family (and a few Mendoza cousins like Walt and Ricardo) climbed into the bleachers. I had my own cheering section in the stands today.

Mom always makes sure I have enough water at games, and I tried to ignore her absence as Auntie Eileen filled that role. Still, the pit in my stomach grew. I plastered a big smile on my face and waved a little too enthusiastically at mi familia, who looked like they were preparing for a rally. They do know how to embarrass me.

#	Player	Position
13	Zoe	SS
25	Sophia	CF
3	Charlotte	1st
99	Destiny	C
5	Kendall	3rd
11	Becky	2nd
10	Yolanda	LF
4	Michelle	RF
7	Teresa	P
-	SUBS	-
9	Lilly	IF
27	Julie	OF

Zoe hit leadoff against the Athletics, but uncharacteristically popped up a slap to left field for the first out.

As I walked up to the plate as the number-two hitter, I heard a roar from down the line. I didn't need to look up to know where the cheering was coming from. It made me smile to think of my squad stomping and hollering, but I had to keep my game face on.

I stepped into the box and pointed the bat toward the mound, almost like a Babe Ruth promise or maybe even a threat. The Athletics pitcher typically throws a first-pitch strike—most likely a drop ball inside. Anticipating her game plan, I set up for a low inside pitch.

I was right. I loaded my body and drove my hands straight to the ball. It felt good initially, but the ball hit the bat too close to my hands and jammed me. I ended up knocking a weak ground ball to second base for an out, instead of a quick fly toward the fence.

What the heck? I knew the pitch was coming, I saw it, I loaded— how did I not send the ball sailing to the outfield? Frustrated, I returned to the dugout and splashed water on my face to hide my disappointment. Rather than draw attention to myself, I slid over to the fence and cheered on Charlotte, who was next at bat. We were three up and three down, and my blood was boiling.

On defense, I slightly redeemed myself by throwing an Athletics player out at third base. She tried to leg out an extra base on a base hit, but not with me in center field. Gotcha!

My next at bat worked out slightly better than my first. Teresa was on base with a double, and then Zoe got on with a drag bunt. I was up with two outs, Teresa on third, and Zoe at first. The As' pitcher wasn't changing her plan too much, so I stuck with my strategy to look low and inside.

The first pitch was up and inside, so I took it for a ball. The next pitch, as expected, was low and inside. Load. Attack. Ouch!

I felt this pitch when I swung, and it didn't feel good. I missed the sweet spot, but was somehow able to knock the ball just out of reach of the second baseman. It wasn't the greatest hit, but I got on base and scored Teresa. We were on the board with a run.

As I tagged first, mi familia went crazy, especially Walt and my youngest cousin April. I beamed at their support, and was happy with the RBI, but still puzzled why I didn't connect well with the ball. I thought about asking Coach, but didn't want her to take it as a sign of weakness. Like Dad says, if you're hitting well, you'll be in the lineup. I didn't want to remind her I wasn't hitting that well for fear I'd end up back on the bench. I needed to get over this slump soon.

My final at bat, I walked and ended up scoring from a pinch-hit by Julie.

"Nice hit, Julie!" I made sure to meet her at the entrance of the dugout to pump her up. She hadn't been in a game in a while, and to have an RBI at bat was huge for her.

"Thanks!" She grinned from ear to ear. I was truly happy for her, and it boosted her morale to be able to contribute to the team.

Final score: Quakes 3—Athletics 1.

After the high-five line with the Athletics, we gathered at a picnic area set up by the parents near the edge of the fields. There were pop-up canopies and foldout tables and a spread of lunch meats and fruit and salad and drinks for everyone. It was a food fiesta.

I grabbed a few orange slices and some turkey, but didn't have much of an appetite because of the heat. Aunt Eileen had a folding chair ready for me and a cool towel to put around my neck. Uncle Joe massaged my shoulders. I felt like a princess!

"Nice game, kiddo!" Joe said. "You made a great catch out there. That was fun to see." It's not just Dad who's a softball freak— all my relatives follow the sport and love to watch our games. They'd stop for a random Wiffle ball game if they saw one being played in a park.

I managed a weak "thanks," but I was tired, the heat was getting to me, and I wished my parents were there so I could let loose with a good whine.

"What's wrong, cochina?" my aunt asked, handing me a paper napkin. I looked down to see crumbs collecting on my jersey.

Apparently old (messy) habits stuck with me.

Aunt Eileen gave me a knowing look, but instead of digging deeper, she took a wet rag and squeezed some water onto my head and neck.

"We'll get you nice and refreshed for your next game. When do you start warming up?"

"In about forty-five minutes. Thanks for coming, by the way."

Watching my younger cousins playing with their mini Wiffle balls and bats brought a smile to my face. Not too long ago, that was Ellie and me at Dad's rec league games. Those are some of the most cherished memories of my childhood, playing at the ballpark with Ellie and Mom and Dad.

Game two: The Cruisers aren't a powerhouse like the Waves, but they're a really fast team, and they know where to tap the ball. Before we knew it, they were "cruising" past first base. We didn't even try to throw them out; they ran so fast, there were no plays to be made.

Each inning, we managed to get one or two girls on base, but we weren't able to group our hits together to push a player home. I walked once, and my other two at bats were meh. Each time I hit, I got jammed. I saw the ball fine, but right when I expected to make solid contact with the barrel of my bat, a sharp, stinging pain shot through my hands and up my arms. The ball ended up dribbling off the bat near my grip and grounding out to second base. Something about my timing was off.

We lost to the Cruisers 4–0. The worst part was that as we clapped hands after the game, I looked up into the stands and saw some of the Waves players. Specifically, I made eye contact with Kristy and Olivia, who were laughing—at us. Then Olivia had the nerve to yell out, "Good game, Lil' Garcia!" It took everything in my power to ignore them and walk away.

Teresa saw the irritated look on my face. "You can't let bullies like that get you down. Just wait. It'll come back to bite them. At some point, we'll show them. It might not be this weekend or even this season, but we'll show them."

"Yeah," I said, but not truly believing it.

⚾

"You sit down and rest, honey," my aunt said as we gathered back at the picnic area for round two of the food fiesta. "And cool off. Your mom will kill me if you get heatstroke!" She scurried off to the food table.

I put a cold, wet towel over my face and closed my eyes. This would be about the time Dad would offer his two cents, and I, of course, would get angry, and we'd probably get into a fight, and Mom would have to come break it up and tell Dad to wait until we got home. Thinking about the scene, I got annoyed because I could visualize the whole fight in my head.

But then the annoyance turned to sadness because although I sometimes get upset with Dad's feedback, eventually it sinks in, and I know he's right. Of course, I would never *admit* that he's right, but I always took his advice anyway.

"Here you go, sweetie." I almost jumped out of my seat when Aunt Eileen came back with a plate of food. I was so lost in my thoughts, I'd forgotten about my hunger.

"Oh, thank you. Wow. That's a real sandwich." The hoagie roll was filled with turkey and salami and cheese and veggies and some kind of sauce, and banana peppers, of course, because I love a little spice.

My aunt pulled up a chair beside me. "That was a tough game. Those Cruisers were good. I can't believe how quick their little feet move!"

"Yeah," I said, disgruntled. "It didn't help that we couldn't figure out how to score a single run. I couldn't even figure out how to get a decent hit."

"Well, you got on base that one time. You know, when you walked," she said, biting into a waxy apple.

"Yeah, I know. But I wanted to hit the ball. And not a little blooper, either. Really hit the ball hard. I wanted to connect with one, and I can't figure out why I didn't."

"I bet your dad would be happy to work with you," she suggested.

"He's never home anymore. He's always working." When that came out, it was angrier than I anticipated. My hand found its way to my mouth, and I chewed on a stray cuticle.

"I know, honey. But I know your dad, and he'll find time. He loves softball, and more than anything, he loves *you*. He'll find time." She reached over and rubbed my back. "You can always talk to Ellie about it too. I bet she can channel what your dad would say."

Aunt Eileen was right. When Dad pitches to us, Ellie and I study each other and try to dissect problems just like Dad would. Dropping your hands? Not loading your legs? Rolling your wrists? I still can't see it very well, but Ellie has gotten good at it.

"Yeah. You're right. Maybe I can talk to Ellie."

Some of the girls stayed later to play Wiffle ball with my younger cousins. It was fun to see my uncle out there coaching the little ones, just like Dad did with Ellie and me. Unexpectedly, another wave of sadness came over me. On the drive home with CJ and Teresa, staring out the window, I wondered if the days of playing ball with Mom, Dad, and Ellie were over. Would that ever be my reality again?

NOVEMBER 14 · PIZZA PARTY

It worked out that Ellie had a weekday game and my parents and I could all go! With our busy schedules, that rarely happens anymore.

Ellie started as pitcher. A huge, toothy smile covered her face when she saw us set up our chairs on the sideline. I forgot how much I love watching my sister play. She is meant to be on that field. Watching her is like watching a symphony orchestra. Her pitching arm wheels around as the ball fires out of her hand. You can hear the pop of the catcher's glove at almost the same moment. It isn't how hard she throws the ball that's so amazing. It's that in a split second, the ball can go up, down, curve out, screw in, rise up. I don't ever want to be a batter facing her as a pitcher.

With Ellie on the mound, the first half inning flew by. Three batters up, three down—all strikeouts. I don't think any girl even got close to fouling it off.

Ellie is not only a great pitcher, she's also the best hitter on the team. She's older than me, so obviously bigger, but she's one of the tallest players her age. Her legs are so long and she has such a wide stance, her feet practically fill up the entire box from front to back. At first, her coaches told her that she would never be a good hitter with a stance like that, but then they saw her hit. That shut them up pretty quick.

Sometimes when you watch hitters, it looks like they're straining every muscle in their body just to get the bat head around. Not Ellie. When she swings, it's like she's holding a plastic bat in her hand. Her hands drive the bat through the strike zone so quickly, it's like she has a superpower.

Ellie bats third in the lineup since she's a power hitter. After the leadoff batter got on base and was bunted over to second by the number two hitter, Ellie had a chance to score her.

It's fascinating to watch Ellie approach the plate. She holds her bat up, looks at the barrel, takes a deep breath, sets her feet, and waggles her bat a few times, then finishes up by pointing it at the pitcher. Her face isn't as intense as I imagine mine is. She has a quiet kind of confidence. That kind of confidence is probably much more intimidating than my glare. She looks so relaxed, like it's Dad out there on the mound during ordinary batting practice.

With a runner in scoring position, Ellie was calm and focused. She took the first pitch as a strike. It was low and away—on the bottom outer corner of the strike zone—but knowing Ellie, that's not what she wanted. She likes them up and in. She took a pitch away for a ball and then another off-speed pitch for a ball. The count was two balls, one strike. The pitcher didn't want to go 3–1 with Ellie, but she wasn't going to lay one right down the middle, either. The pressure was on. The ball was pitched, and Ellie went for it. She sent it sailing into the right-center gap. Her teammate scored easily, and Ellie had a stand-up double, easily running to second base instead of being forced to slide.

The Panthers bleacher roared, but not nearly as loud as we did down the sideline. I whistled as loud as I could, and Ellie glanced our way with a smile and a quick wave. Dad pumped his fist, and Ellie pointed at him like the play was just for him. It never occurred to me that Ellie might be feeling the same way as I do about our parents working extra hours and missing games this season, but their connection today was obvious.

Ellie's team won 6–1. After the game, Mom and Dad took us out for pizza. It's been a long time since all four of us went to our favorite pizza spot, Rock'n Pies. I love going there, because they have a bunch of arcade games we play while waiting for our pizzas to come out of the big brick ovens.

Ellie and I chose classic games right next to each other—me, *The Legend of Zelda*, and Ellie, *Pac-Man*. I don't like the shooting games, but I'm pretty good at progressing through the levels of action games, and I can easily get to level ten on *Zelda*.

I don't think it was the games we were excited about tonight, but the nostalgia. We used to come every Friday for pizza, and Mom would give us four quarters to play. Now we're lucky if we're all home for dinner together. I can't even remember the last time we ate out as a family.

It was the end of a great day, and I wanted Ellie to know that. "It was fun to watch your game and to have Mom and Dad there too."

"I know. I can't remember the last time I saw all of you on the sideline at one of my games. The other team wasn't very good, but we did okay."

"Not just okay, Ellie. You were awesome. I hope someday it'll be as easy for me as it is for you."

"Easy! Who said it's easy?" She paused her game and looked at me seriously.

"Well, you don't seem to stress at all. You walk to the mound or up to the plate like you aren't even worried." I hesitated. "Like somehow you *know* you're going to do well. Don't you ever get nervous?"

"Soph, of course I get nervous. Every game I get butterflies, no matter who we're playing. Like that team today—they weren't very good, but I was still nervous. It's almost like those games are more stressful because everyone is expecting us to win, and it would've been so embarrassing if I didn't play well." Ellie motioned with her hands while she was venting. I guess the pressure gets to her too.

"Well, you don't let it show. You always look so calm and confident."

"Dad taught us that. Fake it until you make it, right?" She nudged her elbow into my ribs with a giggle.

I laughed in response but sobered up right away. My mind shifted to my game last weekend. "But *you* always make it. How long do *I* need to fake it before I make it?"

"What do you mean?" Ellie said, looking perplexed. "Look at what you overcame this season. You started playing for a new team in a brand-new position, and you've already made it into the starting lineup hitting second! I would say you've made it."

"Well, when you put it that way. . . . But it doesn't *feel* that way. Like today when you hit that double, you made solid contact with the ball. I love that feeling and wish I could do it too. But I don't know what I'm doing wrong. I have a plan, I stick with the plan, but every time, the ball just dribbles off of my bat. And Dad wasn't there last weekend to tell me what I was doing wrong, and what's even weirder is that I *missed* that."

We both laughed at the thought of missing one of Dad's lectures.

Then Ellie got serious again. "Look, Soph, softball is a sport about failing. Every player fails most of the time. Do you know what my batting average is?" I shook my head. "I'm hitting .311 right now. That means that I'm basically failing two-thirds of the time."

"Are you seriously trying to make me do math right now?" I asked.

She smiled as she grabbed my shoulders and looked me in the eye to make her point. "Seriously! That's a lot of failure, but it's what we do when we fail that shows everyone, including us, what kind of players we are."

"But I don't know how to fix this problem!" I blurted out as tears welled in my eyes. I averted my head. I *hate* crying, and I *really* don't like crying in front of Ellie because I feel like such a baby.

"Why don't you talk to Dad about it? Go hit some BP. I'm sure he'd be happy to break out the camera and show you what you're doing wrong," Ellie said playfully. We both despised the video camera, but somehow it seemed like a logical solution.

"Okay, I guess I can ask him. It's just that the last time he gave me his two cents, we got into an argument about it. It feels weird to ask him for help now."

"Sophia, if you don't believe you're good, you aren't going to play well." We walked toward the basketball arcade game. "I mean, what did Jimmy Dugan tell Dottie Hinson? 'It's supposed to be hard. If it wasn't hard, everyone would do it. The hard . . . is what makes it great,'" she concluded theatrically.

"Did I hear someone quote *A League of Their Own*?" a voice behind us asked.

Ellie and I whipped around to find Caleb and Alex standing there.

"Oh, hey, Caleb. Hi, Alex." I hoped my voice hadn't quivered.

I looked over at Ellie, who had the biggest grin on her face as she looked from me to the boys. I knew exactly what she was thinking. *How is my sister talking to boys?*

"Um, this is my sister Ellie," I said, trying not to laugh at her face. "These are . . . my friends Alex and Caleb."

Ellie's eyebrows lifted at this interesting new development. "Nice to meet you. So do you guys go to school with Sophia?"

"No, we just school her in sports," Caleb joked.

"Oh, be quiet!" I gave Caleb a friendly nudge. "If you think you're so superior, how about a quick game of hoops?" The arcade basketball game was right in front of us.

Caleb jumped at the chance. "You got it!"

Alex and Ellie were tied basket for basket, but then Ellie took the lead and beat him by four points. She pumped her fist in jubilation.

Then it was time for Caleb and me to compete. I normally am so nervous with boy interaction, but my talk with Caleb at the movies helped me figure out it's not so scary, especially when there are common interests.

We made sure to put our quarters in the slot and hit the START button at the same time. My adrenaline was surging with each ball I grabbed and shot. Ellie was like a hooligan, cheering and hollering behind me.

"My way all day," Caleb shouted each time he scored.

While Caleb was talking smack, I kept one eye on the scoreboard.

I would be up a point, and then he would tie it up. Then he would go up a point and vice versa. It came down to the final few seconds, and I hit a roll—as he hit a slump. I ended up beating him by eight points!

Ellie and I screamed and high-fived each other. Caleb crumbled over the railing in defeat.

"All right, all right. Good game," he said reluctantly.

"What's all the ruckus?" Mom called out as she walked over, interrupting our gloating. "I hate to break this up, but our pizza is here."

"Okay. Bye, Caleb! Bye, Alex. Remember this the next time you challenge us!" I slipped in a giggle as we strutted away.

"You know this isn't over, Sophia. There will be a next time, and we'll totally take you!"

"Never! Girl power!" I yelled, raising my fist in the air. "See ya!"

"Now explain to me what I just witnessed," Mom asked.

"Oh, nothing. Just Sophia kicking her boyfriend's butt in basketball," Ellie said, unable to hold a straight face.

"He's not my boyfriend! I met him last Saturday when I stayed at Teresa's. We talked about baseball and softball. That's it!" I added for extra emphasis.

"I didn't know you had it in you. Good job, little sis. You're growing up." Ellie put her arm around me.

Once my eyes and nose zoned in on our pizza (pepperoni, hot jalapeños, mushrooms, and sausage) I realized how hungry I was. I ate so fast I can't remember if I consumed four or five slices. Just as I started to fade into a food coma, Ellie nudged me and gestured her head in Dad's direction. Ugh. This girl doesn't let up.

I rolled my eyes, sat up, and followed her lead. "So, Dad, we're wondering if you could throw us some batting practice soon?"

Mom and Dad shared a look and tried to conceal their smiles. The smug look on Dad's face was exactly the reason I didn't want to ask for his help.

"Sure, honey. I work a double shift Wednesday, but Thursday we should have enough daylight by the time I get home to throw."

Now it was time for Ellie and me to share a knowing look. "Sounds good, Dad. Thanks!" Ellie responded with enthusiasm while shooting dagger eyes at me. I could tell she was hoping I would be more appreciative, but Mom's and Dad's self-satisfied looks prevented me from being effusive.

NOVEMBER 16 • THE BLOWUP

When Dad got home after a long day at work, he had huge circles under his eyes and looked like he could use a good shave. Ellie and I were so excited to practice that we didn't really process how hard his last few weeks had been. He didn't even have the energy to change out of his rumpled security-guard uniform.

As usual, Ellie hit first. I checked out her routine and hoped that when I was her age, I'd be as good as she is. And hopefully as tall.

After Ellie hit two buckets of balls, it was my turn. I was already out of breath from chasing her balls down, but I put on my batting helmet and stepped up to the plate. Even though I was relaxed with Dad pitching, I still got jammed on my swing. It didn't hurt like it did in my game because Dad throws slower, but that's what was so frustrating. *Dad throws so slow! How could I be getting jammed?*

I stepped out of the box to regroup.

"I think your hands are taking a late load," Dad yelled from the mound. My instinct was to take a deep breath to avert frustration, so I nodded and stepped back into the box. I took in what he was saying and was REALLY trying to concentrate on my hands, but then something else would go wrong and I would pop the ball up or hit a weak ground ball.

Hit after hit, the same thing. Even though some of the hits might have been base hits, I wasn't making solid contact.

"Yeah!" Dad said, walking toward me. "After you load your body, your hands take a second load, which is why you're late on the ball."

DO THIS:

body

First load

He tried to demonstrate, but all I could process was my irritation. I know I asked for his help, and I tried to fix what he was telling me, but it wasn't working. If he's right, why wasn't my hitting improving?

I felt something boil up inside me. I couldn't tell what caused it, but it grew and grew, and before I knew it, I exploded.

"Can you just finish the bucket?" I snapped back. He froze and stared at me for a few seconds

DON'T DO THIS:

hands

Second load

before marching back to the mound. Ellie stopped running after balls to see what the commotion was about. Or maybe she heard and was in shock I would talk to Dad that way. I was definitely blunter than I'd intended to be.

I immediately felt guilty for yelling at Dad. I never raise my voice to my parents, but I was at the end of my rope and beyond frustrated.

My knuckles must have been white from squeezing the bat so tightly, and I was swinging out of my shoes trying to make solid contact with the ball. Blisters formed under the calluses on my hand. But as hard as I worked, nothing helped. Ball after ball just dribbled off my bat.

Dad must have seen how hard and haphazardly I was swinging the bat, and he threw me a changeup. I swung and missed so badly I lost my balance and fell on my rear end.

If I was mad before, I was raging then. "What the heck was that? Can't you see I'm trying my best here? I don't need you to trick me! But I guess you don't care about that. You don't care about us at all anymore. You're never around to care. You never do anything nice for us. Teresa's family does fun stuff together all the time, while Ellie and I are stuck at home cooking dinner for ourselves."

Once I started to rant, I couldn't stop. "Besides, I already have a coach. I don't need another one. Why can't you just be a dad?"

The look of disappointment and hurt on Dad's face was too much to bear. I could feel tears rushing to my eyes, so I tore off my helmet, dropped my bat, and stomped off toward the house.

Ellie yelled to me from the outfield, but tears cascaded down my face, and there was no way I was going back.

When I got home, I went straight to my room and slammed the door. I felt sick about how I treated Dad.

I lay on my bed looking up at the glow-in-the-dark stars I stuck up years ago. *I cannot believe some of those things I said to Dad. He's Super Dad, and I know how hard he works. Why would I say he doesn't care?* There's a part of what I said, however, that has some truth to it. I think the true part is what was making me feel so bad.

I thought back to last weekend, and how upset I was that Dad wasn't at the game to help me, which is incredibly ironic considering I just blew up at him for helping me too much. Then I remembered Aunt Eileen, Uncle Joe, and other relatives showing up as substitute supporters. And how work, and Ellie's softball, and extra shifts always seem to cut into *my* time.

I can't help but compare my family to Teresa's. How great it is to get manicures and pedicures and buy coffee drinks and go to real movies. To not have to share a bathroom or worry about the cost of uniforms or softball gear. How much fun I've had with Teresa and how surprised I was to be able to talk to a boy.

Looking around my room, there's not nearly as much cool stuff as in Teresa's room. My walls are covered with old faded posters of softball and baseball players and mariachi bands. Her walls are covered with nicely framed artwork and pictures of fun family vacations and trips with her friends. We never take family vacations except for camping once at El Capitán State Beach.

After going through it all in my head, I knew what I was feeling: envy. I wished I had all Teresa's things. I wished Mom had time to take me out for manicures and pedicures and buy me coffee drinks every day. I wished Dad made enough money so he could take us on fun vacations to the Grand Canyon and Mexico and Disney World.

Tears filled my eyes as I heard a knock on the door.

"Sophia, are you okay? Can I come in?" Ellie asked.

"I— I— I don't want to talk right now, okay? Can everyone leave me alone for a little bit?" I did my best to not sound like I was crying. I held my breath and wiped my tears away, expecting her to barge in anyway.

Ellie waited a few seconds and then said, "Okay. But I'm here if you want to talk."

"Sure. Thanks." I was kind of surprised she actually listened to me.

I thought back to Teresa's house and how in awe I was of the matching furniture and new kitchen and sparkly pool. How CJ is always available—as both a mom and a coach. Teresa just brushes it off like it isn't a big deal. She actually thought her mom was a little annoying by taking us out the afternoon before the movies. I can't imagine being annoyed by that. If my mom did stuff like that, it would never get old.

When I think about it, Mom would love to do things like that too. She never does anything nice for herself. I don't ever remember her getting her hair or nails done. Despite the fact she's a hundred percent focused on everyone else in the family, I never see her stressed out or depressed. I'm sure she'd like to have all those nice things too, but she never complains. She just works harder and loves on us all the time. Both my parents work so hard just to keep a roof over our heads and food on the table. Lately Ellie and I may have to cook it more days than not, but at least we have food! Now that I think about it, I can't remember the last time I thanked them for that.

The look on Ellie's face at the pizza parlor after Dad said he'd throw us batting practice after a double shift flashed back into my mind. The circles under his eyes and the five-o'clock shadow should have reminded me he hadn't slept in over twenty hours.

Though our families may look different on the outside, Teresa's parents and my parents would do anything for their kids. I think maybe her family and our family are more similar than not.

If I felt guilty before, I feel even more guilty now. I know I have to face my parents and apologize. I can't hide in my room forever. I hate having to say I'm wrong, and I especially hate everyone knowing I'm wrong. It isn't going to be easy, but I have to make this right. The thought of my parents feeling guilty for working too hard makes me sick to my stomach. Now it's just a matter of how to tell them how sorry I am.

ALWAYS BE A
First-Rate
VERSION of YOURSELF
instead of
A SECOND-RATE VERSION
of *Somebody Else*.

Judy Garland
(Dorothy in *The Wizard of Oz*)

NOVEMBER 17 • CASEY TIME

It was a pupil-free day at school today! Unfortunately, it wasn't a holiday for Mom and Dad, so they left for work before we even got up.

Ellie had plans, so I called Casey to see if she wanted to come over. We haven't had much free time together, and I needed some friendly support.

The day was as gloomy as I felt. Unusually gray skies all morning, and it started to rain just as Casey arrived.

"Hey," Casey said as she barged through the door. She immediately plopped on my worn couch and mindlessly starting flipping through one of Ellie's magazines. She's normally really bubbly, talking a mile a minute about some school activity she's organizing or the latest on Jason, but she was oddly quiet.

"Do you want something to eat or drink?" I asked, trying to break the silence.

"Nah" was all I got in return.

After she finished looking at the magazine, she carelessly tossed it aside and let out a big sigh.

"What's wrong?" I asked.

"Nothing. I don't know. It's not really that big of a deal."

"It might not seem like a big deal, but it's clearly got you down. What's going on?"

"Well, yesterday in history class, I was working with Tiffany and some of the other girls. My Vans were muddy, so I wore my Chucks. You know, the ones we painted on my birthday last year?"

"Yeah! I love those."

"Well, Tiffany and the girls didn't think they were that cool. They made fun of me for the DIY fashion. I don't know why it bothered me so much, but I can't get it off my mind."

"No way they were hating on your Chucks! Those are my favorite pair of your sneakers. I remember the day we painted them." I had spent the night at Casey's after her birthday party. We were inspecting gifts from friends and family, and she'd opened the pair of white Chuck Taylors. She put on the high-tops and laced them all the way up.

"Those are sweet shoes!" I said.

"Yeah," she had replied. "They just need—something." Her eyes flashed to the new paint set her aunt gave her. "That's it! Let's paint them!"

"You know you can exchange them for a different color if you want. You don't have to paint them."

"I don't want another color. I want to, you know, *paint* them." She flourished an imaginary brush.

"That's a great idea."

"When have I ever come up with a bad idea?"

"True, true," I said, knowing we'd both come up with some pretty bad ideas in our time. Like TP-ing the Weatherfords' house, only to have to clean up the unfurled rolls of toilet paper the next day. Or the time we drew on each other's faces with permanent markers, pretending it was makeup. Makeup that didn't come off for days.

"Okay, let's do it."

Casey had wanted one side of the shoes to look like a beach, with blue on the bottom (my favorite part) and a mix of colors above that, like a sunset. On the other side, she had painted green strokes to look like a forest and represent her family's cabin in the mountains.

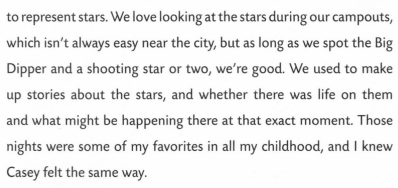

Casey had also painted the rubber toes black with white specks to represent stars. We love looking at the stars during our campouts, which isn't always easy near the city, but as long as we spot the Big Dipper and a shooting star or two, we're good. We used to make up stories about the stars, and whether there was life on them and what might be happening there at that exact moment. Those nights were some of my favorites in all my childhood, and I knew Casey felt the same way.

The heels both had crazy-eye emojis with tongues sticking out. That's the story of our friendship—mucho silliness.

Everything about the Chucks is what I love about Casey.

"It's because they have no idea who you are, Case. They don't get you. I mean, to be honest, all they know about you is that you're a girl who tries to be and look exactly like them. Those Chucks are nothing like them."

She looked down at her lap and sniffed. "To be honest, Sophia, I don't know who I am anymore." I scooted closer to put my arm around her. "I mean, you and Ellie have softball, and you're so confident and have this huge family that's there for you no matter what. I don't have anything I'm passionate about like you do." She paused for a second, and I rubbed her back for support. "And to be honest, I've been worried that I'm going to lose you too."

The real sobs came then, and Casey worked her way through her tears to continue. "You have new friends from your team like Teresa and Julie, and you'll always have your sister and your cousins. I won't have anyone if I lose you."

My heart sank. I knew we'd hit a rough patch since we started the new school, but I guess it affected us differently. I never saw it from her perspective, being an only child and not really having a team to back her up like Ellie and I have. No wonder she's trying so hard with other girls. She's trying to build her own tribe. I thought *I* was losing *her* to this "cool girl" clique. "I'll never leave you, Casey. You're like a sister to me. We might be going through a lot of changes right now, but through thick and thin, family stays together."

"I know. It's just . . . middle school is scarier than I thought it would be. I wanted to make new friends, like you're making new friends on your team. Some friends they turned out to be," she said through more tears.

"That's because they know nothing about the *real* Casey. They don't know how creative you are." I held up her Chucks as proof. "They don't know that you watch most of a scary movie with a blanket over your face. They don't know that your idea of a fun night is camping out under the stars. They don't know how you can recite the dialogue from all your favorite movies. Or that your favorite song is 'Somewhere Over the Rainbow' and how absolutely *horrible* you sing it!" I was hoping to elicit a smile with that, but she still had her face in her hands.

"To be honest, Casey, I've been feeling the same way," I said.

She pulled her head up in shock. "Really? Why?"

"I feel like I don't know where I fit in. My cousin Christina thinks I should be hanging out with her and her Hispanic friends. And then I was scared you're trying to be friends with Tiffany and those other girls, and I have no idea how to be a clone. And my parents have been working so much, and it's been Ellie and me and sometimes just me, without Ellie." I felt tears welling up too. "I yelled at my dad yesterday."

"You what?!" Casey said, shocked. "You never yell at your parents. What happened?"

"It's kind of a long story, but I figured out last night that I miss the way things used to be. It's everything—my family going in different directions, the stress of school, social boxes and trying to fit into one, and boys!" I threw my hands up. "I had a literal temper tantrum—like a two-year-old—because I can't handle all the changes. But I realized that just because other people write rules doesn't mean I have to live by them."

Casey nodded.

"Sure, I have a passion for softball, and I'm part of a big Mexican family, and I'm a movie geek, and I have a sweet tooth, but those things don't define me," I continued. "They're pieces of me—small pieces that make me whole. I have to own who I am and be proud of that."

I could see this train of thought resonated with Casey. Her crying subsided.

"It's okay if you don't have a thing yet, like softball is my thing. We're not supposed to have it all figured out. We're only in sixth grade! I want to be a sportscaster, but that could change. Who knows—maybe I'll become a professional baseball player!"

I saw a smile spread over her face. "You're right. Those girls have no idea what they're missing." She reached for some tissues to blow her nose. Then she grabbed my hands. "Thanks, Sophia. I had no idea you've been struggling with this, too."

"Let's promise to talk it out no matter what," I said, holding out my pinky. We're never too old for a good old-fashioned pinky promise.

"Promise!" she said with a big smile on her face. Then she gave me a hug. A real this-is-just-Casey-and-nothing-else hug.

"So now what should we do?" she asked.

"What do we always do on rainy days?" I asked, hoping she would read my mind.

We smiled at each other and cued up *The Wizard of Oz*. There really is no place like home.

NOVEMBER 18 • COLLEGE GAME

Dad worked late the last few nights, so I still haven't seen him to apologize. I've also been procrastinating because once I start talking, it will all spill out, and the truth will somehow hurt him. But I need to explain myself. It's just a matter of finding the right words and the courage.

I figured I'd do a test run with Ellie. She said Mom's and Dad's work schedules bum her out too, but she won't hold it against them like I'm doing. She didn't make me feel bad about my attitude, but she did make me promise to address it sooner rather than later.

Mom and Dad both worked long shifts today, but I had a valid excuse to avoid the conversation. CJ planned a team outing to a UCLA vs. Notre Dame softball game for inspiration.

We met at Teresa's house. CJ had the dining room table set up with ribbons, glitter, eye black, and temporary hair color. Several team moms set up an assembly line of dining chairs so they could braid our hair. We were going to a college game, and we had to look the part.

Some girls wanted two side braids, some wanted a fishtail braid, and some wanted cornrows. I went with two classic three-strand French braids, one on each side. While getting my hair done and listening to the moms joke with their daughters, I missed sharing the experience with my own mom.

I did my best to stifle my feelings of disappointment, however, and enjoy the moment. We sprinkled glitter and used eye black to write slogans on our arms and faces. I wrote "Go, outies" (short

for outfielders) on one of my forearms, and the other said, "Girls Rock." Zoe's mom put a streak of gold in my hair to match my jersey.

My teammates and I had so much fun getting ready for the game. We had no idea the best part of the day was still ahead.

We arrived at UCLA's Easton stadium to hear the marching band play the "Mighty Bruins" fight song. The place was thumping. When one of our favorite songs, "Can't Stop the Feeling," came over the loudspeakers, Zoe lifted an imaginary microphone and started singing. We all grabbed our pretend mics and fell into imperfect harmony. We danced too, but when Destiny tried her best hip-hop move, she accidentally spun into a young couple with eyes only for each other. We had to stifle our giggles, and CJ signaled us to tone it down a bit.

First stop was the concession stand, where we loaded up on nachos, hot dogs, soda, and candy, which the team covered out of our car wash funds. As we came from behind the bleachers, I stopped in my tracks. The perfectly maintained softball field, massive electronic scoreboard, and seating for more than a thousand fans took my breath away. I almost dumped a loaded hot dog all over myself. Good thing Coach was there.

"Pretty amazing, huh?" CJ said as she grabbed the bun before it hit the ground. "So many great games have taken place on this field. So many girls have sweated through wins and losses here. It's home to some of the best players in softball history."

I scanned the outfield fence and spotted banner after banner for national titles and legendary players. I knew a softball field was more than a pile of dirt, but today, it felt like everything. Mi querencia—my fondness for the sport filled my heart. The game is so much bigger than any one person. Players come to fields like this, at parks and schools across the country, to play the game they love. Each blade of grass represents a play, a hit, a loss, a win. There's something so special about softball. It becomes a part of you. It's much more than glitter, braids, and ribbons. We leave our hearts on the field. We make friends and memories on the field. I thought about my future, and all the memories and friends I'll make someday. It's like the field holds secrets I'm not privy to yet.

"Players leave the field, but the field never leaves them," CJ said wistfully. Her words captured my sentiments exactly.

(My game ticket)

By the time we got to our seats, UCLA was taking the field, and the drumline playing in the stands was so loud it made my heart pump harder. I was mesmerized by the players' precision—it was as if a choreographer designed every step. A Bruins coach hit practice balls so fast, I saw three out at a time. The pop of the ball in each glove synced with the beat of the music. It was a masterpiece of grit and focus, each throw exactly in the right spot. Outfielders took a perfect angle to each ball. Throws to the catcher took a perfect hop. If the UCLA field was an orchestra pit, and the coach its conductor, then her bat was the baton. The girls were so in tune with one another. I thought, *This is what a team looks like in action.*

"They're so perfect."

"What?" Teresa asked, shaking me from my reverie. I didn't realize I'd said that out loud.

"They're so perfect," I repeated. "They haven't missed one ball or made one bad throw. They're like gears, operating in perfect harmony."

"I know. It's amazing. I wonder if those players sat in our seats when they were our age, thinking the same thing."

I was so focused on the pregame warm-up, I hadn't noticed that every one of my teammates was glued to the field as well. Their snacks sat untouched on their laps.

All afternoon, we soaked in every bit of softball we could. UCLA and Notre Dame players hung over the fence cheering as loudly as they could for their teammates. Regardless of the action, they stayed positive.

Each hitter had a focused routine as they stepped up to the plate. Fielders talked to each other after every pitch and hunkered down with determined glares as each pitch was thrown. Players dove left and right. The pitcher moved the ball as if by telekinesis.

It came so fast, I don't know how the batters saw it, let alone hit it.

But boy, did the girls hit. Long ball hitters batted line drives left and right. Three went over the fence for home runs. Slappers had so much control, it seemed they could place the ball wherever they wanted on the field. Soft, hard, chopped, or line drives. And their speed! They flew out of the box and ran through first base in the blink of an eye. The intensity kept us on the edge of our seats.

UCLA won the game 5–2. We lined up along the fence for high fives and autographs. The players were all so nice, and they asked us a lot of questions about the positions we played and the writing on our arms. One of the outfielders saw my left arm and yelled, "Yeah! Go, outies! Don't ever let anyone tell you anything other than outies are the best."

At home, I couldn't stop talking to Ellie about how much fun I'd had at the college game. I replayed every detail. CJ was definitely on the right track taking us to the game, because the only thing I wanted to do besides share this amazing experience is get back on that dirt and get dirty!

Dad would've loved hearing about the game. If he was home, I would've shared all the details of my day and asked him to pitch Ellie and me batting practice. But that didn't happen. And it can't happen. Not until I fix things.

NOVEMBER 20 • THE APOLOGY

Ellie and I found Dad sitting at the kitchen table reading a newspaper when we got home from school.

"Um, I have homework or something I need to do," Ellie said awkwardly, scooting out of the kitchen. "Not here, though. Like, in my room. So yeah. See ya!"

I gathered my courage by taking a deep breath.

Dad didn't seem to take notice when I sat at the table. I cleared my throat, but he didn't budge. I was going to have to start this conversation, so I started simple. "Hey, Dad."

"Hey," he replied without looking up from his paper.

"So I want to talk to you about what happened the other day at practice."

Finally he put the newspaper down and looked up at me. "Ah, I see. Go ahead." He raised his eyebrows while fingering his mustache.

"Well, I, um, I'm really sorry for what I said. I really didn't mean it. I— I guess I've just been going through a lot, and I blew up without thinking." I couldn't even look him in the eye because it was hard not to cry.

"I don't understand, mija. You wanted me to go out and help you, but those things you said were . . . so hurtful. Your mom and I are doing our best with you girls. I was shocked to hear you doubt us. What's going on to get you so upset?"

Those exact words were what I was dreading. That my parents were hurt by my actions.

It took me a second to respond, because I knew how selfish it was going to sound. "I guess there's a lot changing this year, ever since school started. It seems like we were all having dinner together every night, and now it's just Ellie and me most nights." Dad put his huge hand over mine and nodded.

"And school is so different too. Casey and I are having a tough time figuring stuff out, like how to be popular or if we even want to be popular. She's tried to make new friends and got burned by them, and then Christina can't figure out why I'm not hanging out more with her and her friends. And all of a sudden *everyone* has crushes and everyone seems to know how to talk to them but me! I don't want to do what everyone else does, and I don't care if boys like me or not. And on top of all that, softball turned upside down on me. I was supposed to pitch for the Waves, or so I thought, and now I'm playing outfield for the Quakes!" Tears flowed freely down my cheeks. I couldn't hold it in anymore.

"But more than anything, I miss you. I miss Mom. I miss us." Dad moved his chair next to mine and hugged me while he let me cry. It wasn't until we let go that I noticed his cheeks were wet too. I've never, *ever* seen Dad cry before.

"I'm so happy you told me this, " he said. "I know it's been hard for you and Ellie, and I guess your mom and I expected too much of you both. We had no idea you were struggling with so many things. But I can tell you I'm proud of how well you've handled it all. Well, until the other day." He chuckled. I was relieved to hear a laugh. This was a lot of heavy talk, and fortunately Dad is good at knowing how to lighten the mood when things are rough.

"About those girls who are so worried about boys and being

cool and whatever, good for you not wanting to be like them! I'll be darned if my girls blend into the crowd. Look at anyone who is anybody. Do you think they got there by blending in? Heck, no! You do your own thing, and you're darn right you're going to stand out. You girls shine like stars!"

Dad was looking out into the living room like it had magically turned into a podium at the Olympics and he could see Ellie and me standing at the top, collecting our gold medals. Between the smile on his face and the faith in his eyes, I could tell just how much he believed in us.

"Thanks, Dad," I said with a smile, trying to clean up my splotchy, soggy face.

"Even though I might not be around as much as we'd all like, just know how proud we are of you. I mean that. Most kids following in the footsteps of someone like Ellie would have a hard time. I'm proud of you for taking your own path."

The burden of following in Ellie's footsteps was something I never really processed. I saw the questions in people's eyes, wondering if I was jealous of Ellie or had a hard time keeping up. But it never bothered me because I've always felt only pride for her. And I know she feels the same way about me. Now I know that's how Dad feels too.

"So how about we take a look at your videos?" I asked.

Dad's face showed nothing but pure joy.

NOVEMBER 27 · BUCKET RELAY

The Emerald Tournament is the final tourney of the season—a popular showcase held every year near San Diego after Thanksgiving, and a necessary step in moving on to regional qualifiers. It being the Quakes' first year, we didn't get our hopes up. Our goal was to finish out the season and do our best.

Since the UCLA game, the whole team has been working harder than ever. Ellie and I have lifted weights in our garage and taken BP whenever Dad had the chance.

Looking at the game video with Dad, I realized he was right all along. "See! Right there!" Dad paused the video after I loaded my body with the ball coming toward me. And then I saw it. My hands were taking a second load right before the pitch, which made me late on the ball.

"I can't believe it. This whole time you were right." I grabbed a pillow and screamed into it out of frustration.

"You aren't going to have another blowup, are you?"

"No, Dad. No more blowups." I removed the pillow from my face. "But I mustache you a very important question." I laughed. "Why didn't I listen to you?!"

Mom cleared her throat from a nearby chair while she pretended to read a magazine.

"I know what you're thinking, Mom."

"I didn't say anything," she said with a small smile.

"In your defense, Sophia, I know my feedback can be overwhelming, and I'm sure at some point you and Ellie just tune me out." Dad gave Mom a quick glance as she lifted her eyebrows.

"There are some very interesting stories in this magazine," Mom said, aware we were watching her.

"You may as well be reading that thing upside down, caro," Dad joked. He reversed the video to show my stance before the pitch. "See where your hands are when you're in your stance?" They were below my ear and right above my collarbone.

"Yeah."

"When you load your weight back in your legs, you aren't loading your hands." Dad fast-forwarded it to my load. "See? When you start your stance, why don't you start with your hands farther back? Maybe more over your shoulder than your collarbone." He stood behind me and had me get in my stance, then moved my hands, holding an imaginary bat.

"I think this little adjustment will do the trick. Everything else is right. If you get your hands moving *forward* when the pitch comes, instead of moving them back, then forward, you won't be so late on the swing."

Another benefit of being a daddy's girl. No matter the problem, Dad is always there to help me find a solution. He really does know me best.

At our next team practice, CJ focused on offensive strategy by working station to station (one base at a time). To get her point across, she introduced a new activity.

"We're going to have a different kind of competition today!" she began. "Let's split into three teams: Zoe, Sophia, Charlotte, and Lilly on one team. Destiny, Kendall, Becky, and Julie on another team. And Yolanda, Michelle, and Teresa on the third team."

We noticed a half dozen six-gallon plastic buckets placed on the field. Normally the buckets are used to hold practice balls and keep them dry. "The object of the game is to use these bucket lids to move all the Wiffle balls from one bucket to the other as quickly as possible," CJ continued, holding up a lid like a *The Price Is Right* model. "Whichever team wins gets Starbucks drinks on me. Oh, by the way, you also have to touch the lid at all times and keep one hand behind your back."

"All right!" Zoe yelled as our team huddled around our bucket to strategize.

CJ blew her whistle, and when she had our attention, shouted, "On your marks, get set, go!"

Our plan was to have Zoe balance the lid on her knees while she grabbed balls with one hand and put them on top of the lid. She piled as many balls on as would fit. Then she swapped her knee out for her hand, and we took off running. By the time we got to the other bucket, most the balls had fallen off the lid, and we only had two or three remaining to transfer to the second bucket. The other teams were also struggling, and there were Wiffle balls flying everywhere on the field.

It took our team about ten minutes and twenty or so trips back and forth until we moved all the balls from one bucket to the other. Destiny's team finished first, our team was second, and YoYo's team came in third.

We were out of breath but laughing at how hard the seemingly simple task was.

"All right! Congratulations, Team Two!" CJ shouted. Destiny's team cheered and high-fived each other while the rest of us searched for water bottles to quench our thirst.

"What did you learn?" Coach asked, one hand on her hip and the other on her chin, with her index finger tapping her lip.

None of us realized there would be a quiz at the end. But of course, leave it to Zoe to make light of the situation. "I learned my knee can't hold a lid very well," she joked.

"True, true. I took notice of that, too." CJ laughed. "What else did you learn? What changes did you make once you realized your initial plan wasn't working?"

"We couldn't put too many balls on the lid at once," I said.

"So, what worked instead?"

"The fewer balls we had on top, the more likely we were to get all the way to the other bucket," Julie added.

"Precisely! I've been so frustrated because I feel like I've been telling you guys 'one base at a time' over and over, and then it dawned on me that that's all I've been doing. *Telling* you to do it and not *teaching* you how to do it. When you're at the plate trying to score a run, you're piling a ton of balls on your lid—metaphorically speaking. You're trying to do too much. If you can mentally not put so much on your plate, you're gonna end up with more balls in your bucket—or ultimately, runs in a game.

"So today we're going to work on *just* that. We're going to have some batting practice, and our leadoff hitter will try to set the table by getting on however she can. Then the second hitter will move her over, whether it be a bunt, hit and run, or good old-fashioned base hit. Then the next girl will move the runner to third, and the next will hit them in. I'm not looking for double, triples, or home runs. Just one base hit at a time."

It seemed so simple. So logical. But it never really made sense until now. We'd all had the same instinct—to put as many balls as possible on the lid at once. We'd looked so silly trying to recover all of the fallen balls along the way, putting far more effort into the task than necessary. If we'd only taken two or three balls each time, we would've finished in no time.

DECEMBER 2 • MAKING WAVES, TAKE TWO

We've had a pretty good inaugural season: 10 - 2 - 8, winning more games than we lost. Not bad, but probably not good enough to make it to regionals. Our only chance to move forward is to win the Emerald Tournament, a real long shot.

CJ wanted us to scout some of the teams we'll be playing, so we went to a Wolverines vs. Waves game. I heard that Kristy sprained her shoulder a couple weeks ago and was surprised to see her in center field as usual.

The Wolverines are a power-hitting team, known for giving the outfield a serious workout, and it was obvious Kristy was protecting her fragile shoulder. In the first inning, she caught a pop fly, but as soon as she fired the ball to third to stop a runner, she grabbed her arm, cried out in pain, and sank to the ground. My guess is Kristy tore a ligament in her shoulder or her rotator cuff. She was out for the rest of the game, and maybe longer.

Even though I'm not a big fan of Kristy's, it's horrible to watch another player get hurt. A paramedic wrapped her shoulder in a plastic sheet of ice that looked like bubble wrap, but by the look of things, ice wasn't going to remedy the situation.

The most surprising part of the day, however, was when Coach Adam spotted me after the game and signaled for me to come over. I wasn't sure what he could possibly want, and I even looked behind me to see if maybe he was signaling to someone else. I couldn't believe what happened next.

"Your sister Ellie was a star player for the Waves," said Coach Adam. "And we think you can make an impact as well. With Kristy injured, we're going to need a strong center fielder, and I've been watching you all season. I think you'll make a great addition to the team. What do you think?"

"I don't know, Coach."

"I imagine you were disappointed not to make the Waves at the beginning of the season. But now is your chance to join the best team around. And follow in your sister's footsteps. We still talk about what a great player Ellie is."

I was shocked by the offer, but also annoyed that he assumed I wanted to be just like Ellie and that bringing her up would convince me. That was the headspace I was in a couple of months ago, and it surprised me to think how much has changed.

I didn't know what to say, so I told him I'd think about it. As I walked away, Coach Adam shouted after me, "I'll call you later with more details."

As soon as I got home, I rushed to tell Ellie what happened. She was proud (the Waves were, after all, her old team) and told me that all my hard work had paid off. She said it's awesome to be recognized and wanted by other teams, but then she reminded me of a team handout from the beginning of the season and my commitment to the Quakes.

Three Things You Control Every Day

1. Effort
2. Attitude
3. Actions to be a great teammate

Turns out Coach Adam trying to recruit me may be a violation of league rules. Yup—those rules I stuffed in my bag the first day of practice. If the Quakes had finished the season, I'd be a free agent, able to join another team. But since we're still playing, poaching a player is a direct violation of league rules.

Coach Adam promised Dad in a phone call that the rules can be bent, but we said no anyway. I was so happy the Waves wanted me, and it made me feel good that Coach Adam realized his mistake in letting me go, but I love playing for the Quakes and would rather play for a team with integrity than win a championship. Two paths I could go down, but in my heart, I knew what I had to do.

December 9 • EMERALD TOURNAMENT, DAY ONE

I was bummed no one in my family could come to the tournament with me, but when I opened my bat bag, I found a note and a candy-filled survival kit from Mom to cheer me up.

FireBalls: To keep you fired up throughout the game

Tootsie Rolls: To help you roll with the bad calls

Mints: To keep you cool under pressure

Baby Ruths: To remind you to hit like Babe Ruth when you're up to bat

Candy Hearts: To show you how much we love you

Mom knows me so well.

There were at least twenty teams participating in the two-day Emerald Tournament, with double elimination rounds and stiff competition. Base by base, game by game, the Quakes rallied. We were dirty and sweaty and worn out when we found ourselves, once again, up against the Pacoima Pumas. This was a must-win game if we wanted to stay in the tournament.

CJ posted a new lineup.

#	Player	Position
13	Zoe	SS
25	Sophia	CF
3	Charlotte	1st
99	Destiny	C
5	Kendall	3rd
11	Becky	2nd
10	Yolanda	LF
7	Teresa	P
4	Michelle	RF
-	SUBS	-
9	Lilly	IF
27	Julie	OF

We knew from our last loss against the Pumas that they were a tough team, and not surprisingly, it was a tough game. We couldn't get anything going, and it all came down to the bottom of the seventh. The game was tied 0–0 and we were up to bat. Teresa led off with a hard ground ball hit between third and shortstop. Julie came in to pinch-run so Teresa could save her energy in case we went into extra innings.

Michelle, batting ninth, laid a beautiful sacrifice bunt for an out but successfully moved Julie to second. Then our rotation started over, and, leveraging our short game, Zoe slapped the ball for a base hit to move Julie over to third. We had a runner at first and third, one out, and it was my turn at bat. My heart raced as I stepped up to the plate. I glanced over to CJ, who gave me a slight nod of reassurance.

Just like Dad and I practiced, I took my stance and made sure my hands were over my shoulder. I glared down the pitcher, doing my best to intimidate her with my game face. I visualized holding a lid with one ball on it. Walking calmly and smoothly, moving the single ball into the bucket.

At the same time, an image of Dorothy clicking her heels together three times popped into my head. I hoped the same magical power the clicks gave her in *The Wizard of Oz* would help me get around the bases—all the way home. Instead of actually clicking my heels, I hit them three times with my bat.

It made me think about my family, how much I love spending time with my sister, and how whole they make me feel. Especially being here alone today, I was hoping for a little bit of comfort, encouragement, and magic to spark up my bat.

The first pitch was up and in, which I would have swung at if I was trying to hit a bomb. But not now. I was calm. All I needed was to get the ball through the infield. Just like CJ said. No pressure of a double, triple, or home run. Just through the infield. I looked for something low so I wouldn't pop the ball up.

I took a deep breath before the next pitch. The chatter from both dugouts and the bleachers faded out as I zoned in on the pitcher's hand. *Focus on the ball*, I told myself. The pitch came in low, just like I hoped. I drove my body, hands, power, and faith right at that bright yellow ball and smacked it directly to the pitcher. She ducked just in the nick of time, and the ball skittered along the ground toward center field.

Julie immediately took off from third base and ran flat out. The Puma catcher could only watch as she safely stomped home plate for the score.

Our dugout and fans roared in celebration. The Quakes funneled out of the dugout for high fives and hugs. We won the game! We did it together as a team, one base hit at a time. We were moving on.

December 10 · EMERALD TOURNAMENT, DAY TWO

Even though it was a surprisingly warm day for December, I felt a chill realizing my family wouldn't be in the stands for the last day of my regular season. I'm used to their absence, but it didn't make it any easier.

We were all jittery during our first game and lost to the Choppers by one run, which meant we needed to win at least three more games to stay in contention.

The loss whittled away at our self-confidence. We didn't believe we deserved to be there, or had a chance to win, or move on to regionals.

CJ reminded us otherwise. "You can't judge the entire season on one game. You girls earned your place here. We've worked hard all season, and when other teams gave up, you fought harder."

Then she held up her cell phone and said, "I've got a surprise for you."

Suddenly Lauren's face appeared on the screen, live from Michigan. "Ohmygod," she squealed. "I'm so happy for you guys, and I wish I was there!" We pushed in so she could see us all.

"Sophia, I hear you're crushing it in center field!" Lauren laughed. "Who would've imagined you'd be playing outfield? I guess you all don't miss me *too* much!"

"We miss you," the whole team shouted in unison.

"Anyway, just wanted to wish you good luck. I'm playing for the Ann Arbor Aces now, but I'll always be a Quake at heart. I'm rooting for you!"

⚾

The next games were against the La Verne Lions, the Temecula Tigers, and the Bakersfield Bears, and we headed onto the field with a boost of confidence. The first two games were tough, but with Teresa's dominance on the mound and Char's hot bat, we were unstoppable.

Scores:

Quakes 3—Lions 2

Quakes 1—Tigers 0

Like most players, I'm superstitious, so when something's working, I don't want to change it. That's why I decided to repeat the same routine as yesterday. The next time I was up to bat, I knocked my heels three times with my bat. And guess what? I got another base hit. And then another. And another.

We then put up a late fight to shock the Bears and rallied from a three-run deficit to defeat them. Every single person on the team, whether they were on the field or on the bench, contributed. We were on a streak after three consecutive wins and actually had a shot at winning the whole tournament!

Resting under a canopy, waiting to find out the winner of the other elimination round, I heard a whistle. An unmistakable whistle. Dad *did* make it!

I looked across the field to see my WHOLE family trek across the parking lot: Dad, Mom, Ellie, and Casey along with aunties, uncles, Christina, and at least five younger cousins laden with supplies. I was surprised to see Casey walking alongside Ellie and Christina, and even more surprised Casey and Christina were getting along. Maybe Christina had started to appreciate Casey's loyalty, which trumps any cultural barriers. I know I appreciated seeing them. Softball really wasn't their thing, but they were there to support me. I caught their eye and enthusiastically waved.

Saying my family packed everything but the kitchen sink would be an understatement. Unloading picnic baskets, coolers of bottled drinks, containers filled with cut-up fruit and cheese, plastic tubs with guac and salsa, and giant bags of chips, they looked like they were settling in for a long haul, rather than one game. They even brought my favorite tamales. Casey made a point to bite into one with a huge thumbs-up and a roll of her eyes that said, *I'm in heaven!* It was like my abuelita was there too. I'm not sure if it was all the Mexican food my family brought, or the music blaring from Christina's wireless speakers, or the general camaraderie, but I was fully revived and ready for the fifth and final game.

As fate would have it, we had some history with the winner of the other bracket. Yup. We faced the Waves for the championship game. It was like a Hollywood movie—a showdown between archrivals. (I may be overdramatizing things here, but I felt like we were Team USA vs. the Russians in ice hockey during the 1980 Winter Olympics. *Miracle* is another one of my favorite movies!! ♥)

The Waves strolled onto the field with a cocky attitude. Kristy, still on the DL, had her arm in a sling, and I heard she's recovering from surgery. I'm not sure if she knew Coach Adam tried to recruit me for her position, but I avoided making eye contact with her anyway.

Right out of the gate, the Waves scored two runs at the top of the first inning. Olivia, who moved into center to replace Kristy, hit a double down the right-field line. It wouldn't have bothered me if it were another player. There's just something about Olivia that rubs me the wrong way—the way she and Kristy were so rude and condescending to me at the tryouts, and the way they laughed at me after our loss to the Cruisers. CJ was right; there're definitely teams and players that don't know good sportsmanship.

CJ checked to see if Teresa was tired. It was her fifth game of the day, but I saw her adamantly shake her head all the way from the outfield. She was going to stay on that mound until the end, and I think that's exactly what everyone on the team wanted too. We had to complete some unfinished business.

Once out of the inning, CJ spoke to us in the huddle. "There's no other team out there that can do better when their backs are against the wall. The Waves think they have this in the bag. Look at them." We glanced over to their dugout. They were going through the motions, grabbing their gloves and walking out to their positions, laughing and goofing off. We don't even look that lackadaisical at practice. In their eyes, we weren't a threat.

"Do they look intimidated to you? They aren't even taking this game seriously. If I were you, I'd be angry. You love this game. You *respect* this game. So get out there and show them how it's done!"

"Yeah!" the whole team simultaneously roared.

Yolanda led the charge: "'Fight' on three. One, two, three—"

"FIGHT!" we screamed.

Zoe was up first, and she slapped the ball perfectly between third base and the shortstop. Then I was up, and as much as I would've loved to knock a home run over Olivia's head, I reminded myself of our plan—station to station. CJ gave me the bunt signal.

I took a deep breath and tapped the heel of my cleats three times. *Get the ball down,* I thought. The first pitch was a rise ball so I laid off, not wanting to pop the bunt up. The third baseman charged in quickly and stayed close to me. I slyly glanced at the first baseman, and she didn't seem to move at all—she held pretty far back, close to the base.

The last thing I wanted was to bunt it right to third base and have her throw Zoe out at second. I had to go for first base.

The next pitch was out, but I went for it anyway and

managed to get the barrel of the bat all the way around to lay a bunt down between the pitcher and first. The two Waves players miscommunicated, and neither one of them fielded the ball until it was too late. I ran past the bag, and Zoe raced safely to second.

Charlotte hit a deep fly ball to left center, and Zoe and I were able to tag up and advance. Then Kendall hit a base hit to right center, which scored both Zoe and me.

Just like that, we were tied 2–2.

Coach Adam had no intention of letting an upstart team overshadow his, so he filled his batting rotation with power hitters. By the top of the seventh inning, we trailed the Waves 3–2, and they had a runner on first with two outs. We were running on fumes.

The number-two Waves hitter poked what seemed to be a routine fly ball to Yolanda in left field. I thought YoYo had it until I saw her take an angle that was far too short. I took off toward the ball because I knew she was going to miss it. I slid on the ground like I was sliding to a base to cut the ball off, grabbed it, and then threw as hard as I could to second.

The Waves runner slid forcefully into the bag, and it was tough to tell the call from my vantage point.

"Safe!" the umpire yelled.

The Waves roared up against the fence. Then they all hopped onto the bench and continued cheering. One of the girls grabbed two balls and started banging on a bucket to the beat of the "TRUCKIN'" cheer.

T-R-U-C-K, keep on truckin' all the way.

T, T-R-U, T-R-U-C-K, keep on truckin' all the way!

The Waves seemed more into their cheer than sealing the win. With the end in sight, they thought they had the game in the bag.

My heart beat in my ears. No way! She was out! Well, at least I really wanted her to be out.

The Waves now had runners on second and third, and my heart stopped when I saw who strolled up to the plate next. Olivia. I looked over to Teresa on the mound, and she returned my gaze.

"Two down!" She pointed her two fingers at me with determined eyes. "We got this, Quakes! Tough D!"

I pointed my two fingers back at her, reassuring her that we had this. She knew how I felt about the Waves, and Olivia in particular, so I'm sure she wanted to give me an extra boost of confidence.

The first pitch was a ball, and seeing the smirk on Olivia's face made me rage. Teresa was tired, and the last thing she needed was this girl taunting her.

Teresa's next pitch was a rise ball. She was trying to get Olivia to pop out. Unfortunately, Teresa's arm wasn't as strong as it had been earlier in the day, and the pitch was a little flat. She piped it right down the middle of the strike zone, and Olivia unleashed on it.

The ball was coming right at me. Well, not quite right at me—in my direction, but over my head. I dropped back and sprinted toward the fence. Going back to one side or the other is a lot easier than straight back, but I didn't have that luxury. All I could do was

run as fast as I could, while trying to keep my eye on a ball 3.8 inches in diameter soaring high above me through the sky.

I was gaining on my target. I had a shot. At least, I felt like I had a shot until my cleats hit dirt—the warning track. I was running out of space. *But I was almost there!* I jumped and stretched my glove up as far as I could reach.

My body bounced off the fence and hit the ground. Blurry vision made the next few seconds difficult, but I looked in my glove and saw a bright yellow ball in it. I raised my glove for the umpire to see. I officially robbed my first home run!

I stood up with my glove still held high. My team ran out and tackled me like we had just won the World Series. Everyone was screaming, my family in particular, and I heard Dad's voice above the crowd.

I'm not sure if it was me being a little dizzy from hitting the ground or if I was in complete shock, but it felt like I was dreaming. Like I was having an out-of-body experience. Like I watched someone else make the play because it couldn't possibly be me.

Then I realized it was real. It was me. *That just happened!* I let out a big "YEAH!!" with a fist-pump to the sky. It was better than any strikeout on the mound I ever had as a pitcher.

"Holy cow! Who are you?" Teresa said, shaking me. "You looked like Caitlin Lowe out there." I blushed as I remembered my conversation with Caleb.

Going into the bottom of the seventh, the Waves still didn't appear worried. They seemed confident they could hold their lead. Michelle led off the inning and poked the ball between the third baseman and shortstop again, but the shortstop made a good backhand play on her for the out.

Zoe didn't falter and followed up with a great at bat. I think her at bat tallied fourteen pitches! She just kept fouling balls off, making the Waves' pitcher, Amanda, more and more tired until her final pitch ended up in the dirt and Zoe made it on base with a walk.

Then it was my turn. One out, bottom of the seventh—the last inning and our last shot to win the game. I was going to have to get something going. Teresa wasn't going to be able to hold off their hitters if we tied it up and went into extra innings. It was now or never.

Before the inning started, CJ had told us that the Waves' pitcher didn't want anyone to really connect with the ball, so she'd probably work on keeping the ball down and out while mixing in off-speed pitches.

Breathe. Inhale. Exhale. While looking at the barrel of my bat, I thought of Ellie, and her calm confidence that I saw in her games time and time again. I slowed my heart rate down by taking some deep breaths, trying to channel that confidence. I closed my eyes and told myself, *You have a plan. Think low and outside. You're going to have to go opposite field. You got this.* As I stepped into the box, instead of glaring at the pitcher, I kept my face calm and tapped my cleats three times.

CJ was right: first pitch was low and outside, exactly what I was looking for. I made sure to load my hands and body back early so my hands wouldn't hitch back late. I threw my hands at the ball and . . . didn't feel anything when I made contact. The ball exploded off the barrel of my bat, skipping off the grass into the left-center gap. Before I put my head down to run, I saw Olivia making good ground on it. *I don't care who she thinks she is—I'm making it on base!*

Olivia cut the ball off from going to the fence. Zoe got a good jump, and Olivia could see she had no play on her going to third base. Her only play was me, wheeling my way toward second. She was getting her legs under her to throw the ball for an out. I channeled all my inner strength, hoping my legs would move just a little faster. I slid into the bag and simultaneously felt a hard tag on my chest.

"Safe!" the umpire yelled.

A surge of satisfaction and relief charged through me. I wanted so bad to throw that same grin at Olivia that she threw at Teresa, but I needed to focus my attention on my team. I clapped, and a puff of dust rose from my hands.

"Let's go! Come on, Quakes! Let's do this!" I yelled toward the dugout. My vocal cords were giving out from all the cheering today. Our team was beside themselves in the dugout, going wild, and my family was even wilder. I think even the kids playing Wiffle ball nearby stopped their game to watch.

I loved that Charlotte was up next because she's our most consistent hitter. She usually finds a way to get on base. Coach Adam called a Waves timeout. I hustled over to meet up with CJ, Zoe, and Char.

CJ said, "Remember, she's going to keep the ball down because she'll want to take away the long ball. Just one hit at a time, Charlotte. Sophia, sweet hit, by the way! Now be smart out there. Zoe and Sophia, don't get picked off, and don't go taking off with the ball in the air. Stick with our plan."

We hustled back as Coach Adam walked by. He took his cap off and wiped his brow. I could tell from his expression that he wanted the game to be over.

Amanda's first pitch was in the dirt and outside. The second pitch was an off-speed pitch, for a ball. That's pretty dangerous to get behind in the count with Charlotte up.

The next pitch was low and more or less down the middle. Charlotte connected with it and sent it flying right back to the pitcher, who was barely able to get out of the way.

Zoe took off and ran her heart out. She danced over home plate, and we were tied!

I rounded third base with no destination in mind other than home plate. I could tell CJ was thinking the same thing. She was jumping up and down, waving her arms. The only thing between me and the win was the Waves' catcher, Kim. She was totally blocking the base path as Olivia threw the ball in—a hard, perfect hop right to her. My best bet was to go around her.

I started to break right. I could see Kim lunging toward the ball. My side hit the ground as I flipped onto my stomach and stretched my fingers out to swipe the plate. Kim never even touched me. The crowd went bananas. I didn't need to look up because I knew I was safe.

We won!

My team rushed out of the dugout and tackled me again. I was

covered in dirt, and a bunch of sweaty, smelly, screaming girls were lying on top of me—but I couldn't imagine any other place I wanted to be.

Yay, team, whatever it takes,

We represent the championship Quakes!

I felt like I landed in another mosh pit when my family surrounded me with congratulatory hugs and high fives. Dad, especially, had *I am proud of you* written all over his face. Christina, Ellie, and Casey came up together with such enthusiasm, you'd think they were meeting Beyoncé or something.

"That was so amazing!" Casey said, hugging me. "I need to come to more games if they're all this exciting."

"I'm pretty sure this white girl just came for the food," Christina teased as she nudged Casey. "Girl can eat! Ya know what I'm sayin'!" I was beginning to wonder what planet I was on that these two were not only getting along but teasing each other and laughing together.

"Yeah. I couldn't help myself. Christina and I were talking about hanging out at the skate park tomorrow. I hope you don't have plans because you're coming. I'll bring bagel chips!"

"Sold!" It was great to see my family and best friend getting along so well. I guess when you just get to know a person for who they are and not who you think they are, you might surprise yourself. Maybe even make a friend or two.

"Wow, Sis." Ellie came up and put me in a headlock. "I mean, wow. I've never seen a team fight so hard and work so well together. You really have something special. You're lucky. And man, I don't even want to start with you because then it will go to your head, and I'll have to beat you up a few times to snap you back into reality." She fake-threatened a noogie and let me go. "Seriously, though. I'm proud of you."

"Thanks, Sis." And I gave her a big hug.

CJ was surrounded by an enthusiastic Quakes team chanting, "SoCal Regionals! Here we come!" when Teresa broke away and ran over to her bat bag. She pulled something out and put it in my hand. I looked down to see a gold charm necklace identical to the one she wore.

"This couldn't be more perfect for you," Teresa said as she clasped the chain around my neck.

Just then, my little cousin April ran over to me with an oversized baseball cap on her head and a big smile on her face. "Sophie, you're my most favoritest player in the whole world! I hope I can be a center fielder like you someday!" she said, tossing a Wiffle ball in the air.

I had to stop a second to process what she said. She's just a little girl, but she said something big league. It made me realize something. That's how I used to look at Ellie. She's always been my most favorite player in the world. I idolized her. I wanted to be just like her. That was a huge part of why I wanted to be a pitcher and why I was so disappointed when I felt like I was failing at my dream of becoming her.

It took those words from my five-year-old cousin to show me I'm not Ellie. I'm not some person trying to live someone else's dreams. I'm living my *own* dream, and doing a pretty good job of it. Maybe I'm a natural just like Ellie is a natural. A natural . . . outfielder!

I can't wait for postseason!!!!

GLOSSARY

abuela: *grandmother* in Spanish

ball: a pitch where the batter does not swing, yet the pitch is outside the strike zone (too high or low or not over the base)

barrel: sweet spot of the bat

batter's box: rectangular area beside home plate where the batter stands while at bat

BP: batting practice

bunt: a ball intentionally hit softly so it's difficult to field

changeup: a pitch meant to look like a fastball, but slower—short for "change of pace"

chopper: a ball hit into the dirt in front of home plate

clutch RBI: a run batted in when the score is either tied, or your team is losing

count: the number of balls and strikes a player has in their current at bat

crow hop: a forward leap an outfielder makes after catching the ball to gain momentum to add power and distance to their throw

curveball: a pitch that curves or breaks from a straight path toward home plate

DL: disabled list

double play: two outs made at a time

doubleheader: two games played back-to-back

drag bunt: a bunt hit on the run

drop ball: a pitch that starts straight and dives as it reaches the plate

dugout: where a team's bench is located

extra innings: when the game is tied, additional time added to determine winner

fastball: common pitch that is thrown more for high velocity than for movement horizontally or vertically

fielder's choice: when a runner safely gets on base only because a defender chose to make a play on another base runner

fly ball: ball hit high in the air

gap: space between outfielders

grounder: a ball hit on the ground

inning (7 in softball): a period in which two teams alternate between offense and defense, and each team is given three outs

line drive: a hard-hit ball that is neither a fly ball or a ground ball—more of a straight line

load: the transfer of energy from legs to torso, using momentum to fuel the swing

masa: *dough* in Spanish

pinch runner: a substitute who comes in from off the bench to base run for a player who has gotten on base safely

pinch hitter: a substitute who comes in from off the bench to hit for another player

pop fly: a ball that isn't hit very far in the air—most likely in the infield or in foul territory

RBI: runs batted in

rise ball: pitch that starts out mid-height and rises up

shallow outfield: space between the infielders and the outfielders

short game: bunting and slapping

shortstop: the defender that plays between second and third base

slapper: a fast left-handed hitter who predominantly relies on short game to get on base

stand-up double: when someone gets a hit and easily reaches second base without needing to slide

strike zone: the space above home plate between the batter's knees and the midpoint of their torso

utility player: a player who can play multiple defensive positions

windup:

Ball release

Phase 1   Phase 2   Phase 3   Phase 4   Phase 5   Phase 6
Wind up   6 o'clock   3 o'clock   12 o'clock   9 o'clock   Follow through

ACKNOWLEDGMENTS

We are so grateful for the love and support that came our way during the writing of *There's No Base Like Home*. We would like to thank all the librarians, teachers, and booksellers who advocated to get this book into the hands of young readers; Jane Schonberger and Pretty Tough, for seeing the need for great stories of strong female athletes; our publisher, Stacy Whitman, a true advocate for diverse voices; and our family, who inspire us every day and are the backbone of what made this book. Lastly, to all the young girls that will grow up to be strong women: You are our future. Our reason for writing this book is for you, to help you find your strength and lead the world around you.

ABOUT THE AUTHORS

JESSICA MENDOZA is a Major League Baseball analyst for *Sunday Night Baseball* on ESPN. She is the first female analyst in MLB postseason history and ESPN's first-ever female MLB analyst. Jessica also serves as a contributor on ABC's *Good Morning America*. She won gold & silver Olympic medals in 2004 and 2008, respectively, as a member of the US Women's Softball Team. Jessica's younger sister, **ALANA MENDOZA DUSAN**, was a Division 1 softball player at Oregon State University. She currently teaches high school English and lives in Bend, Oregon, with her husband and two children. This is their first novel.

ABOUT THE ILLUSTRATOR

RUTH MCNALLY BARSHAW is the award-winning author and illustrator of the *Ellie McDoodle* series. She played softball for a summer league when she was twelve, but learned much more about strategy from this manuscript. She resides with her author-husband Charlie in Lansing, Michigan. See her work at www.ruthexpress.com.